D is for Dog: dogs in hea
by
David Holmes

Prologue

The Labrador retriever limped across the dry grass, favoring its left hind leg and sat before his master, big brown eyes watching intently as Rodrigo's large hands moved over his double coat from his wide flat head to the broad chest and along his flanks.

"Maybe you aggravated that old injury while climbing the hillside behind the old olive tree. "What do you think, Blackie?"

Blackie thumped his long tail twice on the hard ground. Panting from the exertion on a warm day in early September, the dog's pink tongue hung from its mouth, the white canines shiny with saliva.

Rodrigo patted his dog's head and scratched behind the large, floppy ears. "You're almost ten years old now, boy. You first hurt that leg when you were only four and it's always healed up in two or three days."

The wind blew particles of dirt across the unpaved driveway of the caretaker's cottage and stirred the brown grass between olive trees in the grove below the small house. Overhead, fluffy white clouds passed in the pale blue sky, typical for Andalusia at the end of summer/beginning of autumn. The worst of the heat was gone. The rains of October were still weeks away.

For nine years, since turning twenty, Rodrigo had lived in the white stucco cottage on the edge of the estate of Don Miguel de Goya, his employer, east of the vineyards of El Condado and a few miles north of the marshlands of one of Spain's finest national parks—a place of adventure and great delight for him and his dog. Though Blackie was trained to retrieve, Rodrigo did not hunt waterfowl with his dog.

Don Miguel de Goya was a distinguished Spanish gentleman, a man of wealth with a variety of business interests—mostly legal—in the southern province, with headquarters in Seville. His international ventures often involved smuggling certain agricultural products out of Morocco and across the Strait of Gibraltar, though he strictly avoided anything derived from opium...a matter of principle and honor. Don Miguel had come to depend on Rodrigo, who performed the duties of bodyguard, enforcer and general persuader to those reluctant to see things the way of his boss.

In these days of global trade, Rodrigo's fluency in English, sort of, made him even more indispensable. It should be noted that Rodrigo had learned English while living with his sister in Brooklyn, so his manner of speech was different to that spoken at Oxford or Yale. On the estate, Rodrigo seldom ventured to the main ranch house, a sprawling one story affair constructed with Moorish influences—outdoor fountains and patios with flowers and fruit trees.

Rodrigo was not married nor did he have a regular girlfriend. His last serious love had left him abruptly for a vacationing German businessman and, much as he had tried to, he simply could not blame her. Blackie the dog remained his best friend and loyal companion.

Once again, he patted the blocky head. "It's gonna be all right, big guy. We'll see Doc Sanchez. He'll make you feel better."

Blackie lay down and rolled onto his back, inviting a vigorous tummy rub.

"Ah, you're a good boy!" Rodrigo said, and scratched the dog's chest and belly.

Chapter 1

One week later

"How long has Blackie been lame?" the elderly white-haired man asked.

"Eight days since the latest episode."

"So, it has lasted longer than before." The vet adjusted his white lab coat. "He is nearly ten?"

"What are you saying, Doc? A friend's chocolate lab is almost fifteen and still retrieves birds."

Blackie started panting and moved around as the vet palpated the animal's hind legs. "The old x-rays revealed little. Perhaps a soft tissue injury like a muscle strain was to blame. This time a sprain is more likely, since ligaments do not receive a strong blood supply and take longer to heal. I want to take more x-rays, all right?"

"Whatever you think is best, Doc. I always pay my tab."

"We don't worry about the money. We are here to serve God's creatures."

"Whatever it takes to fix him..."

A young female assistant came into the exam room and hooked a leash to Blackie's red collar. As Rodrigo stood by the empty exam table, she noted his above average height, sinewy muscles, strong face, dark eyes and full head of black hair. She had heard the other assistants speak of his former career as a professional boxer in Europe, a ranked light-heavyweight when he'd retired from the sport. Then she remembered the dog and looked away, leading Blackie toward a back room and the x-ray machine.

"You want me to come too, Doc?"

3

"Have a seat, Rodrigo. I'll show you the film when we are done," Dr. Sanchez said, and left the room.

Twenty minutes passed and the vet returned. "Come with me," he said, and led the way to a small room with a computer monitor on the wall. The elderly man typed on the keyboard and brought up a black and white image of a dog's hind leg.

"Fortunately, we are not dealing with hip dysplasia." With the sharpened end of a pencil he pointed to the knee joint. "Like a human's, but different, so bear with me. An injury to the meniscus might be causing the lameness. For the most accurate pictures I will need to sedate him in order to position him on the table. In most cases, I can surgically repair ligament injuries though, afterward, you will have to rehab him carefully."

"I'll follow all of your instructions, Doc," Rodrigo promised.

"However," the vet pointed at a white splotch on the lower leg, "there is another possibility...a very serious one."

Rodrigo stared at the image on the monitor. "The bone looks okay to me."

"It could mean osteosarcoma. I can't be certain yet. Take Blackie home. Bring him back in a week and I will take more pictures. Can you do that?"

"Anything for him, Doc. Just tell me what to do." Rodrigo looked behind at his dog, waiting in the doorway. Suddenly his heart felt heavy. "Is he gonna to be all right?"

"If it's bone cancer..." Dr. Sanchez sighed. "Let's hope for the best and not worry about the worst. I want you to give him the pain medication I am prescribing, twice a day. Blackie is tired and anxious now, so go home and let him do what gives him pleasure."

Rodrigo tried to smile. "Thanks, Doc. You've always helped him."

Chapter 2

It was a fine day in mid-September as Rodrigo stepped from his cottage, a cup of strong black coffee in one hand. The scorching temperatures of summer had abated and he looked up at the clear sky and saw a cloud in the shape of a dog. Maybe I'm just seeing what my eyes want to see, he thought, or maybe God is thinking of Blackie too. On cue, Blackie appeared and stood at his side.

"How's the appetite this morning, big guy?"

Seven days had passed since the visit to the animal hospital and the dog seemed to have lost interest in eating—never a good sign. For the first time, Rodrigo noticed that Blackie's broad head was no longer flat. There were obvious contours on both sides of the crown of the skull. Rodrigo's eyes also noted the appearance of atrophied muscles at the dog's back end, weight loss that had occurred since the last appointment.

Things had gotten to the point where Rodrigo had to entice the dog to eat by placing morsels of food in its jowls. Only then would Blackie begin to munch. It was a time-consuming process, but Rodrigo didn't mind if it helped his sick friend.

Fortunately, the dog still drank plenty of water, often from the hose his master held while watering terracotta pots of flowers. Don Miguel's wife had insisted that he adorn the whitewashed walls of his cottage with colorful plants—carnations, roses, jasmine and geraniums.

As an ex-boxer Rodrigo was careful with his weight and kept a portable scale. Stepping on it, the readout stopped at 175 pounds, normal for him since his fighting days. He bent down, lifted Blackie and stepped back on the scale. The combined weight registered at 240 lbs.

The vet's scale had given a reading of 70 lbs. just a week ago. He set the dog down. A loss of 5 pounds in a week was unusual, Rodrigo realized.

As the dog brushed past him and walked out to the fields to do his business, Rodrigo saw that he was reluctant to bear any weight on the left hind leg, causing Blackie to walk a bit sideways. Accustomed to danger and dealing with hard people, Rodrigo seldom felt fear; however, looking at his beloved companion he had to admit that he was afraid. It was a vague unarticulated fear that now stirred in the back of his mind.

Suddenly the telephone rang and he reached inside the door of the cottage and took the receiver. "Yeah?"

"Barquero here," the caller announced. Juan Barquero, Don Miguel's chief lieutenant, was in charge while the Boss was in London for a medical procedure. "Got a job for you. Come to the office in an hour and I'll give you the details."

"Mr. Barquero, I got a sick family member. Can't Carlos handle it?"

"Yeah, I heard about your dog. How's he doin'?"

You can't keep anything secret in this organization, Rodrigo said to himself. "Not too good. He needs lots of care."

"Come in to Seville anyway. How about getting someone to dog sit for you?" Barquero said, and hung up.

What I need is one of those sabbaticals the professionals get, he thought. God knows I've earned a break. Watching his dog cross the reddish dirt driveway back to the cottage, Rodrigo asked aloud, "Who can I call?"

Mrs. Moore was usually available. She was an Englishwoman recently retired from a British-owned sherry bodega at Jerez de la Frontera and lived a couple of miles east. Then he recalled hearing that she was on holiday in Eastern Europe. That left Maria, who assisted in Don Miguel's kitchen; except, her duties precluded an open-ended commitment. No one else had any experience with caring for Blackie overnight.

The phone rang again. "Yeah?" he answered abruptly.

"Is this Rodrigo de Lorca?" a young woman asked in English.

Irritated, he said, "You're the one calling. You should introduce yourself."

The girl laughed. "Does the name of Jamie Hayden mean anything to you?"

"Who is this?"

"A friend of Jamie's and his friend...one known as the Little Doctor of Casablanca."

Remembering his adventures with the young American—son of a U.S. government intelligence agent—and the medical doctor, a Berber woman named Soraya, Rodrigo relaxed. "You're the Goth, that Moroccan girl?"

"Samantha Zafzaf, at your service."

"How you doin'?"

"Terrific. Can we get together for lunch?"

"Where are you?"

"Seville, near the cathedral."

"Okay. I gotta take care of some business this morning. At one o'clock, take a taxi to Pulpitos. It's a tapas bar in the La Macarena quarter close to El Rinconcillo, supposedly where tapas were first served in the 17th century. The driver'll know the place, so don't let him take you for a ride."

"Don't worry about me. Streetwise is my middle name."

After saying goodbye, Rodrigo called the main house and asked Maria, the assistant cook, to come down and watch over Blackie for a few hours. He leaned down and rubbed the dog's ears. "Sorry, old friend, I gotta go into the city. Drink some water for Maria, okay. I'll be back as soon as I can."

Chapter 3

Rodrigo parked his car near the Iglesia de San Pedro in north Seville, the same quarter he'd told Sami about, and walked to an office building on the Calle Regina. The receptionist waved him through to Juan Barquero's ground floor office. Dressed in a dark blue suit, Juan Barquero sat behind a large wooden desk. As Rodrigo entered, he gestured to the younger man to take a seat on the other side of the desk.

"Would you like some coffee?"

"No thank you, Mr. Barquero."

Barquero glanced sharply at his Rolex and spread open a manila folder on his desk. "I will get straight to business then."

Rodrigo wore his favorite light grey sharkskin suit with an open-neck light yellow shirt. Black loafers protected his feet. He didn't wear a watch; rather, he kept an old Timex in his jacket pocket. "Should I take notes?"

"For you, no need. Your memory for faces and facts is well known."

Rodrigo rolled his neck, nodded. His mind was on his dog.

Barquero laid three color photographs on the desk, next to the computer monitor. "The fat one with a round face is Pedro Jaca. He owns a shop selling leather goods, mainly to tourists, in the Santa Cruz quarter. Very lucrative for Senor Jaca, except he likes to play the horses. And," Barquero scratched his large nose and ran a hand over his dark, thinning hair, "he is not winning these days. El Gordo—the Fat One—took out a loan from Garcia and is two months overdue."

"Got it," Rodrigo said.

"Next, we have this guy in the middle, Jorge Blanco." The photo showed a middle-aged man of average build with a long face and a neatly-trimmed mustache, wearing a suit and vest. "Senor Blanco is an accountant for Repsol, but we can skip the oil company connection. This is personal. Blanco's wife is from a wealthy Madrid family. She is accustomed to a certain style of living. When Blanco failed to secure an expected promotion, he also paid a visit to our friend Garcia. The wife isn't supposed to know the true state of his finances, nor would her family help if they knew. Word is, they did not approve of the marriage. As I speak, Jorge is three months in arrears."

"The last guy resembles the actor, Ricardo Montalban."

"Dani Montesa. Opened an upscale restaurant in the El Arenal quarter last year. Got off to a good start, very popular with the international set. Then a few months back, there were cases of hepatitis A in the city, which the municipal health authorities traced back to an infected cook at Montesa's establishment. Business fell off like Atlantis disappearing into the sea."

Barquero had received his education at the Universidad de Sevilla and was not shy about letting his rougher-edged peers know it by dropping erudite references into his conversation. "Senor Montesa feared losing his restaurant and prevailed upon Garcia to "invest" in the eatery. But a month ago the place closed anyway. Maybe he used the money for investments elsewhere, like out of the country."

"Why can't Garcia's people collect?"

"As you know, they usually do when the clients are in Seville or, at least, in Andalusia." Barquero tapped a fountain pen on the photos. "These men, evidently, have left the province. We have reason to believe Montesa has fled east to the Costa Blanca, somewhere in the vicinity of Alicante or Valencia. He may have family in Barcelona."

"So he's number one?"

"He owes the most money," Barquero said, and gave a thin smile. "Next, Pedro Jaca was last seen heading north, perhaps to Castilla-La Manch, or maybe the Extremadura."

"A big area. Anything more specific?"

Barquero shook his head sympathetically. "Have a look at the file before you leave. Our sources indicate Jaca attended the university in Salamanca for two years before dropping out. Oh, and for a foreign language, studied Portuguese."

"The province on the Portuguese frontier, the Extremadura. That's the place to start."

"Finally, there is Senor Blanco," Don Miguel's lieutenant said. "The accountant was last seen driving northwest out of Madrid. He may have altered his appearance." Barquero put down the pen.

"They all possessed passports?"

"Yes. We checked with the issuing authority. A search of their residences indicates they took them. On the other hand, they must know we have people watching airports, train stations and overseas ferry terminals."

"The borders with France and Portugal stretch for many hundreds of miles, more often than not in mountainous and isolated countryside. As for our long coastline, whether the Mediterranean or the Atlantic, any fishing village presents a way out."

"Still, these men are middle-aged city dwellers. They are not outdoorsmen or men of adventure."

Rodrigo stood up. "I will find them. I just wanted to point out that we are a nation of almost fifty million and these are three men with a whole country to hide in. By altering their features, even a little, it might be enough to allow them to slip through your net of official and unofficial watchers."

"For this task, I share Don Miguel's trust in you. You are like what the Americans call a bounty hunter. You possess the skills to track down these men and bring them back to Seville or...to make an example of them. You understand what I am saying?"

Rodrigo scooped up the photos, put them in the folder. "Let me study this for half an hour. I will leave it at the front desk."

"Anything you need, tell me."

"Money," he said without hesitation. And then an idea came to him. "And the RV."

"Oh?" The firm owned a Mercedes-Benz high roof van, professionally converted into a recreational vehicle with a kitchenette, bed, dinette, and wet bath with toilet and hand held shower. It was used to deliver Moroccan-sourced products throughout the province—innocent enough looking when driven by one of Don Miguel's older employees and the man's crippled-by-arthritis wife.

Barquero reached into a desk drawer and drew out a set of keys. "Take care of it. It is Don Miguel's pride and joy."

Chapter 4

Tapas, an old Spanish tradition in drinking and dining.

Outside Pulpitos, Sami was a sight to behold in her black blouse, black slacks and shoes, long black hair and black lipstick, in addition to the mascara on her long, thick eyelashes. She lit a cigarette and stared boldly back at gawking young Spanish males passing by, saying nothing—letting them know, with a subtle shake of the head, that she wasn't available.

When Rodrigo walked up to Pulpitos he was taken aback. Here was a full-bodied young woman with round, dangling gold earrings, a golden nose ring and eyes that would stop a thief in his tracks—the left orb blue, the right one brown.

He gave a short bow. "Your eyes, they are truly extraordinary. You are wearing contact lenses?"

She shook her head, fluttered her eyelashes. "You must be Rodrigo."

"A woman as perceptive as she is pretty. Shall I call you Samantha?"

"My friends call me Sami. As for my appearance, you're not the first guy to comment on that. Are Spanish men always on the make?"

"You mean the men of Morocco are not?"

Laughing, she dropped her cigarette and crushed it with her shoe. "I'm hungry."

"Me, too. I'm buying, so let's eat."

They went to up to the bar and ordered. Beer for him, red wine for her. The first plates of the day's snacks—tapas—were set on the bar and, without conversation they sampled the *calamari fritos* (batter-fried tentacles and squid), chunks of *chorizo* (garlic and paprika-flavored sausage), *patatas bravas* (pieces of spiced potatoes) and *Jamon Serrano* (thinly sliced ham, salt-cured in the nearby mountains), followed by a few mouthfuls of green olives and fried almonds. Their portions were added up and noted for the final bill. Rodrigo ordered seconds on the drinks and led Sami to a quiet corner table, away from the glare off the older whitewashed buildings across the street. The early afternoon crowd was filtering in and the noise level increased.

"Had enough?" he asked.

"Very tasty. I love the custom, picking a bit of this, a bit of that. Altogether it makes a meal. By the way, what does pulpitos mean?"

"Baby octopus." Rodrigo lifted his bottle and took a long swallow. "So, tell me, why are you here?"

"Ben Jelloun asked me to perform a favor. I couldn't refuse him, he is like an uncle to me."

Rodrigo nodded solemnly. "You are referring to the Jewish hunchback, Don Miguel's most reliable source for a certain product from your country. You must have demonstrated that you are worthy of Ben Jelloun's trust."

"You could say that. He knows what I am capable of," she said, and drank some wine. "By the way, I turned eighteen today."

"Then this is a kind of celebration. A very happy birthday to you, Miss Zafzaf." He raised his glass in a toast. "Our friend, Jamie-boy, said that he owed his father's life to you."

She smiled. "As an American, Jamie tends to exaggerate."

Rodrigo pulled his old watch from a pocket and sighed. "I'm sorry to rush things, but I've been given a job that will take me away from Seville. As a result, I must find someone to care for my dog." He shrugged. "It is rude of me to—"

"I finished my work for Ben Jelloun this morning. Now I am free." She emptied her glass. "Since I'm not in a hurry to get back to Morocco, let's have a look at your dog. You're talking about a few days?"

Rodrigo brightened. "You would do that for me?"

"For your dog," she corrected. "I love animals."

He got up, left money on the table. "Can you drive?"

"Can dragons fly?"

"Pardon?"

"It's a saying. Of course I can drive. Stick-shift, automatic, car or truck...I can handle it."

He handed her the keys to his car. "Did you bring any luggage?"

"Just this." She lifted an oversize leather bag. "I travel light. I always buy what I need locally."

Impulsively, he took her hand and kissed it. "You are a gift from God."

"Wow, no one's ever said *that* to me before."

"Come. You can follow me in my car. I will be driving a red Mercedes van...an RV."

"Isn't that for old people?"

"Only in America. Anyway, I *am* old compared to you. I am twenty-nine."

"Where are we going?" She took out another cigarette and her lighter.

"I live on Don Miguel's ranch, west of the city." On the sidewalk, he squinted in the midday sun and put on a pair of sunglasses. "Now my heart is at rest, knowing Blackie is in good hands. You're sure you don't mind staying with him? I mean, he is ill and needs a lot of attention."

Sami paused, put the cigarette back in the pack and put away the lighter. "Your dog is sick?"

"Don't be scared. He can still walk—"

"No, I just meant that I'd better give up smoking for a while. Better for the dog. Maybe better for me, too."

Rodrigo exhaled loudly. "You had me worried for a minute."

"Say, I've got a great idea. Since you're so worried about your dog, why not bring him along?"

"Travel with Blackie?"

"Exactly. A road trip with a dog," she said and giggled.

"But it is a kind of business trip."

"Your dog doesn't know that. Imagine...you, me and Blackie, on the road to adventure!"

Rodrigo rubbed his chin. The more he considered what sounded at first like a wild notion, the more sense it made. Suddenly, he cupped her face with his strong hands and kissed her cheeks. "Sami Zafzaf, you have saved *my* life. I will forever be in your debt."

"Hah! Careful what you promise."

Chapter 5

At his cottage, Rodrigo packed hurriedly, throwing clothes and toiletries into a battered brown Samsonite suitcase while the cook, Maria, put together a light meal for dinner.

Outside, the red van glistened in the afternoon sun. As Sami got acquainted with the dog, Maria carried a bulky basket of provisions into the RV. She placed the perishables in the small fridge, the rest in a small pantry.

Inside the cottage, Rodrigo opened the top drawer of his bureau and lifted a blued 9mm semiautomatic pistol, started to ram a loaded magazine into it, and then stopped. This time it must be different, he decided, without fully realizing why.

He had operated before off hunches and had learned to respect them when they occurred. He put back the gun, covering it with a red bandanna. At that moment, Blackie limped into the front room, followed by Sami.

"So you two have met?" he said, and carried his luggage to the door.

"He only barked twice, so I think he must like me a lot."

"Sorry, but he only barks once at people he really, really likes."

Sami looked crestfallen.

"No, no. Can't you see I am only kidding? He trusts you to follow him already."

"Have you trained him to heel?"

"He will walk at my side, not for anyone else. He is very protective of me."

Blackie barked.

"A good family dog always is," she agreed.

"Listen, Blackie, this is Sami and she is our new friend." The dog wagged its tail. "Want to go for a car ride?"

Blackie barked again.

"Then let's go!"

Rodrigo guided the dog to the van and lifted Blackie's hind legs up and into the RV. A pair of folded wool blankets lay on the floor next to a counter, directly behind the driver's seat, forming a bed for the dog. After sniffing around the van, Blackie lay down on the makeshift bed, curled up and watched his master load the luggage.

"This is the short wheelbase version," Rodrigo explained. "It's got the 3.0 liter V-6 engine, a turbodiesel." He waved an arm around the interior. "We've got 2 single beds at the back, so nothing awkward in the sleeping arrangements, if you know what I mean."

"Everything is copacetic."

"Huh?"

"It's fine, Rodrigo. Don't worry about a thing."

"Okay. Well, the tall cabinet behind you contains a wet bath—toilet and a handheld shower in a fiberglass shell. And, on my right, the counter, sink, fridge and a two-burner stove. Uses propane."

"Like travelling around in a small apartment."

"That's it exactly. And with the high roof," he looked up, "we won't bump our heads or have to hunch down. It's a real class ride. What do ya' think, Blackie?"

"Arf!" the dog said.

"There's also air-con, and a furnace if the nights get cold, say in the mountains." He got down on his knees and stroked the dog's back.

"I think we're ready to go," she said.

Rodrigo closed the sliding door on the passenger side and they climbed into the cab of the van. "First, I gotta find a guy named Dani. This is confidential stuff, okay? I know I can rely on you to be careful with the info."

"I'm nothing if not discreet."

He looked at Sami, her dark clothing and make-up. "Yeah, I can see that. Anyway, this fella owes money and he's gonna have to pay it back with interest. He knows it, we know it. That's how it works. Nobody gets a free ride here...bad for business."

"We're talking about a loan shark?"

"The guy owed money is a businessman," Rodrigo corrected. "One of our contacts last spotted Dani near Murcia. Question is, where'd he go from there? Some say Alicante, on the Costa Blanca. Lots of tourists there, so maybe he'll try to bum a ride with one. Then there's Valencia up the coast. Easy to lose himself in the crowds or take a ferry or private boat ride to the Balearic Islands and mix with foreigners on Ibiza and Mallorca."

"Why would he trap himself on an island?"

"He owned a restaurant in Seville and a lotta tourist types were customers. Plus, the guy could be a double for that Latin actor, Ricardo Montalban. Foreigners eat that up...you know, posing for photos with Dani Montesa like he's the famous guy himself."

Rodrigo started the diesel and let it idle on the driveway, a panoramic view of rolling hills and olive groves through the tall windshield. He unfolded a paper map. "Spain. He could be anywhere in the country. Since our source pinpointed him in Murcia, that's where we're going first."

He pointed a finger at a city in the southeast. "A guy who does odd jobs for us spotted him in the Plaza Santo Domingo, near the cathedral. He was getting into an old car—like a taxi, but not a taxi."

"Meaning what?"

"The driver is probably from a nearby village, providing cab service...one without a meter."

"Legal?"

Rodrigo shrugged. "That's how it's done here."

Sami reached into her bag, took out a cellphone and punched in a number. "Ruben? This is Sami Zafzaf. I need some information." She described the subject and the place where he was last seen. "Call me back soon with the info. I'm heading in your direction."

"What was that about?"

"You've got your people, I've got mine. We'll pool resources."

Rodrigo glanced over his shoulder at the dog. "Time to hit the road, boy," he said, and released the parking brake. Putting the vehicle in drive, he took it slowly down the hill to the road that led to the motorway.

Chapter 6

Decision time loomed near the international airport east of Seville. Take the southern route on the A92 motorway through Granada along the Sierra Nevada range and over to the Costa Brava or head northwest on the A4 to Cordoba, paralleling the Guadalquivir River and, eventually, into lower Castilla-La Mancha province?

Or through Granada, former capital of the Moorish kingdom in Spain to Murcia near the coast, about 300 miles, with another 100 miles north to Valencia? The route that passed near the fabled city of Cordoba to Valencia was roughly 350 miles.

Sami's phone rang. "What've you got, Ruben?" The Goth listened intently, then said, "Okay, thanks," and turned to Rodrigo. "Your actor look-alike was just seen in Valencia, leaving a small hotel near the Plaza del Ayuntamiento. He was wearing a straw hat and aviator-style sunglasses, but it's definitely him."

"Then we take the A4," Rodrigo said, and followed the road sign northward to Cordoba.

"How long before we get there?"

"Hard to say exactly. Something like four hours should do it." He reached back and touched his dog. "Blackie'll need breaks, just like us."

Golden hills lined with row upon row of olive trees marched across the countryside, replacing the cityscape, the thrum of tires and the quiet rumble of the turbodiesel filling the van. The heat of the day increased and they raised their windows and enjoyed cool air from the air-con unit.

Eventually Sami caught a glimpse of the Torre de Alminar, the 305-foot tall bell tower of Cordoba's cathedral, known as the Mezquita—built originally as a mosque in the year 785. But they didn't stop for services, trusting to the van's extended range to reach Valencia by late afternoon.

When Rodrigo heard Blackie's restless movements he pulled over at Montoro, a small city on five hills with a 15th century stone bridge over the Guadalquivir. Within sight of the town's typically Andalusian whitewashed buildings with red tile roofs, Rodrigo helped his dog down from the van and, on a leash, walked him around.

Carefully, Blackie sniffed for the correct place to pee. Duty done, he drank water from a ceramic bowl and chewed a handful of dry food as the small chunks were slipped inside his jowls.

Sami spread a bath towel on grass by the van and, while the dog lay down, went to the small fridge and took out two bottles of orange juice and gave one to Rodrigo. After quenching her thirst, she asked, "What makes you so sure this Montesa guy and the others won't have fled the country before you can locate them?"

"They are not professional criminals, they are businessmen—hardworking and intelligent—who made some mistakes, borrowed money and think they can't pay it all back." He swallowed some juice.

"Think they can't?" she repeated.

"I've hunted down guys like this before. See, they fall behind on their payments, the interest rate is high and they panic. So instead of going to Don Miguel and asking for an extension, they skip out on the loan. What's so unusual this time is that three men of Seville took off within days of each other. But, believe me, they aren't running toward a life of poverty. They always stash something away to start a new life. Those investments are what Don Miguel will persuade them to forfeit in exchange for safe conduct and a return to their old lives in Seville."

"Persuade them? Isn't that putting it mildly?"

"Okay, so I've done some rough stuff before. But only with guys that deserved it. They asked for the money, agreed to the terms. They gotta pay up. That's the way the game is played."

"What'll you do to Senor Montesa when you find him?"

Rodrigo paused to drink up his juice. He wiped his mouth on his sleeve, let the bottle dangle from his hand. "Normally, I'd bend a thumb too far or maybe shift a kneecap. Nothing too serious...just enough to inflict a bit of pain, get the guy's complete attention and reorient his focus away from running to paying what he owes.

"Now," he looked down at his dog, "I don't want to break any bones, not with him along. It's hard to explain."

"I think I get it. Bad luck spills over and you want Blackie to recover."

"Something like that," he admitted.

"Okay, one more question. Isn't this red van kind of high profile? You know, different enough to tip off the runners?"

"Yeah, the color does make it stand out. Still, it's an RV and nothing more at this point. Usually it's driven by an old man, one of Don Miguel's cousins, on delivery trips around the province. The holding tanks underneath the chassis are modified. There's the standard freshwater tank and a black water tank for the toilet.

"But the gray water tank from the sink and shower are diverted to the waste water tank, allowing for a hidden compartment to carry certain items, free from inspection."

"Very clever," Sami said admiringly.

Rodrigo helped his dog stand up by lifting its back legs. Once more, he noticed the atrophied muscles at Blackie's hips and rear and swallowed hard.

"You okay?" she asked.

He ignored the question. "I don't care if the runners notice us. As a matter of fact, I *want* them to know I'm after them. They're amateurs at this and when they feel pressured, they'll make mistakes."

Back on the road, vast fields of cereals alternated with citrus trees in the river valley. Then the road curved gradually to the north, the sparsely-settled hill country of the Sierra Morena rising up on their left.

The history of the towns along the route often carried as far back as the days when Carthaginians, those great traders of the Mediterranean, ruled much of the area. Their famous general Hannibal, he of the army with elephants that crossed the Alps and invaded Italy, defeated Rome's allies on the Iberian Peninsula.

But winning battles in Hispania eventually cost Carthage their hold on the peninsula, as Rome struck back hard in the Second Punic War. And with the arrival of the highly-disciplined Roman legions onto the Iberian Peninsula, Rome's skilled engineers built bridges and aqueducts, and plotted and laid down roads in Andalusia.

Besides the influence of ancient Rome, the land reflected the many centuries of Moorish rule, longtime inhabitants of southern Spain after crossing the Strait of Gibraltar from Morocco in the initial burst of conquering frenzy by Islamic tribes. Their architecture—the columns, geometric designs, fountains and gardens—had left a permanent mark on southern Spain.

By mid-afternoon, the Mercedes van was had crossed into the province of Castilla-La Mancha, the wide plains filled with grazing cattle, medieval castles on hilltops, fortified cities and the tall and white, cone-topped windmills that were reminiscent of Don Quixote's quixotic quest with his faithful squire, Sancho Panza—Cervantes' enduring literary masterpiece of Spanish language.

Rodrigo turned northeast onto the A43 motorway for the second half of the journey to Valencia and the Mediterranean coast. While Sami unbuckled her seatbelt and climbed back to the kitchen area to make sandwiches, he considered the fate of his dog. He should have taken Blackie back to the vet for more x-rays, he thought. Then again, he was scared of what the doc might find.

Of course, there was always a chance it wasn't too serious, he told himself. But he'd read up on the worst outcome. All the experts had all noted that by the time an accurate diagnosis was established, the cancer would likely have already spread—metastasized, they called it, an evil word by any spelling and in any language. Rodrigo decided that, after grabbing the film star's body double, he and Blackie'd go back to Doc Sanchez' clinic and face whatever it was like a man.

Or a dog.

Chapter 7

The sight of fruit orchards alerted them to the nearness of Spain's third-largest city even before reading the road signs.

Bright orange orbs hung heavily in the midst of green leaves and, with windows down, the fragrant scent of the citrus meant that they were close to their destination, with several hours left to find a place to park the van before nightfall. Strictly speaking, Spanish laws required RVs to park overnight in an official campsite.

As the motorway approached the coastal city, the usual industrial blight—business parks with glass and steel buildings, long metal warehouses and distribution centers with ramps for articulated trucks—littered the landscape.

Rodrigo pulled off the divided highway and coasted to a petrol station's diesel pump. After filling the tank he drove the van over to a grassy verge and parked. Sliding open the side door, he half-lifted Blackie down and let the dog walk unleashed.

"He's gotta take a leak," he explained matter-of-factly.

"According to this," she held up her smartphone, "there're campgrounds near the sea."

"Watch him," he said, gesturing at the dog. He went inside the van, opened a cabinet and pulled out a pair of magnetic signs, two feet by three. He fixed one to the passenger's side door and the other on the driver's side.

Sami got down and read aloud the black words on white background, "Pablo's Custom Motorcycle Parts. Jerez de la Frontera." Taking a brush, she ran the soft bristles over the dog's glossy coat. "What if someone calls your bluff and wants to order something for his bike?"

Rodrigo went back to the cabinet, took out a paper catalog and tablet computer and held them up. "It's no bluff. The business is real, one of Don Miguel's legitimate enterprises. Pablo can fabricate anything for motorcycles—exhausts, aluminum luggage, engine cases, you name it. With this tablet, I can take an order and send the request from anywhere in Spain. Hopefully, not on this trip. The signs on the doors turn the RV into a commercial vehicle so we can park in the city without attracting police attention.

"Incidentally, Spaniards are insanely crazy about motorcycle racing. Valencia has a racetrack that hosts a round of top level MotoGP racing every year. We'll fit right in." He returned the tablet and catalog to the cabinet, opened the small fridge, took out two plastic bottles of bubbly mineral water and passed a bottle to Sami.

She put down the brush and drank some water. "He's a magnificent-looking animal. His thick double coat keeps him warm and dry even in marshlands, right?"

"You got it."

"And large webbed paws for swimming out to retrieve ducks?"

"I trained him to retrieve, but not waterfowl. I don't hunt animals." Rodrigo stared at his dog. "His claws are huge and they're so hard, you'd need a grinder to trim them. I just leave them alone."

Blackie looked up at his master and blinked, his big brown eyes seeing everything. "Give him some water, without the bubbles, while I check the map for a downtown park."

"I can find it with my phone's GPS."

He shook his head. "I'm a little old-fashioned about these things. I've never gotten lost, at least not yet." He went to the wet bath and closed the door. Coming back out, he zipped up and spread his map on the small counter. Finally, he circled a spot with a pencil.

Dog at her side, Sami stood at the door. "What'd you decide?"

"Jardines del Rio Turia, a six-mile long public park in the old city, on the site of a dried-up river. We'll try for a place not far from the cathedral in the old city center since Montesa likes to mingle with the tourists."

"What if he took a ferry to the Balearics?"

"I gotta guy watching the terminal. Believe me, Montesa is here. I'm sure of it. Come on, let's get Blackie aboard."

Even in the heavy late afternoon traffic, it wasn't long before he saw the landmark. "From where you are sitting, the Miguelete's at the two o'clock position," he said, and pointed through the windshield. "That's the bell tower of the cathedral."

They found an open spot to park opposite the long greenbelt, a place that would also serve Blackie's needs. Before leaving the van, Rodrigo took time to feed his dog, slipping dry food into his mouth and waiting patiently for the dog to crunch down with his powerful teeth. "Doc Sanchez said his breed were 'garbage dogs' because Labs'll eat anything, anytime. Except now it's a chore for him. It's like he's lost interest in eating."

Sami squatted on her heels. "Animals are smart. They can sense what's going on inside themselves. Sometimes they just shut down if the injury or illness is serious."

"That's enough, Sami!"

Recoiling, she held up her smartphone. "Mind if I take pictures of him? You know, in case—"

"Let's change the subject, okay?"

She cleared her throat. "All I meant is... if you misplace your camera, I'll have photos of him."

Sighing, he took off his sunglasses, wiped his eyes with the back of his hand. "Sorry, I'm on edge. It's the allergies this time of year."

"Sure. The pollen bothers me, too."

"So, what's the deal with the black wardrobe?"

"Right, I dress like a Goth. It's more an attitude than a style of dress for me, though. I've been on my own for a while."

"What about family? Spaniards are big on family."

"Dad's a Vietnam vet. After that war he decided most Americans were Chickenhawks and settled in Morocco, married a local lady, and here I am."

"Chickenhawk?"

"You know the type—my country right or wrong, 'we support the troops' patriots waving the flag on bridges and trucks and Harley-Davidsons. They're the biggest boosters of war, but the least likely to actually serve and do the dirty work. Dad said there's a lot of money in making war, not so much making peace."

"Sounds like a wise man. The Golden Age of Spain—the 15th and 16th centuries—was fueled by gold and silver from the New World. Our conquistadors destroyed the Incan Empire and stole their gold, then enslaved the Indians and forced them to labor in silver mines.

"The money financed the king's wars in Holland and Belgium, which drained the treasury until the country went bankrupt. All that stolen South American wealth was squandered making war. People don't learn and they don't really change. Thank God there's always some who try to do the right thing, regardless of the cost to them."

"How can *anyone* know what should be done?" she said.

"We all got a conscience."

Chapter 8

"We can't leave Blackie in the van. It's too hot," Rodrigo said. "Put him under the trees. He can lie on the grass," Sami said. "I'll watch over him while you're gone."

"Good plan. I'll ask around, check with my contact. We'll find the movie star."

"Sure. But let's face it, you're distracted right now."

"That's putting it bluntly."

"It's not meant as criticism. Blackie's on your mind, not this scumbag Montesa." She looked across the street. "Over there, the curb and sidewalk are covered in red goop."

He followed her gaze. "La Tomatina, at the end of August. We just missed the largest tomato throwing fight in the world. Thousands take part. They wear old clothes and toss ripe tomatoes at each other. The red fruit of the vine are brought into the city by the truckload."

"Fantastic! Can you imagine pelting the girl—the one who just dumped you for a rich guy—in the face with a juicy red one?"

"I wouldn't do that to her."

"Did I touch a nerve? Okay then, how about nailing a Mr. Perfect with a big fat red one between the eyes and watching the juice and seeds slide down his startled face? You know the type—upper-middle class family, professionals, big house in a respectable neighborhood, finest schools, great career, vacation home, investments, good health, beautiful wife? Yeah, hit him right smack in his 'full of himself, spoiled brat' eyes, that's what I'd like to do."

"You got a big streak of mischief, Sami-girl," he said and smiled.

At least I brought him out of his funk, she told herself. "Okay, go and look for Montesa. Blackie will be fine. We'll have a picnic, won't we boy?"

The dog stared at her, expectantly.

"Any trouble, anything at all, call me." He lifted the dog down onto the grass and gave her a key for the van.

She led the dog several yards into the park and spread a bath towel under the shade of a tree. Blackie tried to pee before laying down, but nothing came. She brought his water bowl. When he wouldn't drink, she scooped up handfuls of water which he licked from her small hand.

"Good boy," she said quietly. "Blackie's a good dog."

Rodrigo gazed at his dog for a minute, then walked into the old city. Passing in front of the cathedral he examined the crowds of foreigners coming and going, singly and in groups. The area he wanted to cover was compact, perhaps half a mile from the church to Valencia's main train station, which was where his local informant kept watch.

If he was honest with himself—and he tried to be—Rodrigo would've admitted he was in no hurry to apprehend Dani Montesa. Because then he would have to return to Seville and the animal hospital and he was afraid of hearing the vet pronounce a final verdict.

For a moment, he was nearly paralyzed by the fear of losing his dog and gulped several deep breaths in the Plaza de la Reina behind Valencia's cathedral. Walking on, he strolled across the square wearing slacks and long-sleeve shirt, his suit jacket draped over his right shoulder.

His feet were cushioned from the rough pavement by rubber-soled black loafers. Lace-up shoes would have been more secure if chasing human prey, he thought; however, these guys were in their forties and not, according to the file, men of action. He figured that he could walk faster than they could run.

As he moved through the narrow streets from the Central Market to a museum and then another church, he listened to a babble of conversations in German, French, English, and Italian. Even though August had passed—the main vacation month in Europe—there were plenty of people on holiday. Didn't anyone work anymore? he wondered.

No sign of the failed restaurateur at the usual tourist destinations, so he headed for the railway station next to the Plaza de Toros. The station had been built over one hundred years ago in the Art Nouveau style and featured sculpted orange blossoms on the outside and murals of orange groves. Well, Rodrigo decided, I'm partial to Seville oranges.

Then he recognized Sesos, his contact. In a manner of speaking, the man fit the name. He was of slight build, wore reading glasses and had a neatly-trimmed goatee with an unlit pipe jutting from his thin lips. An unlikely looking petty criminal, Rodrigo surmised, and not at all like his predecessor in Valencia, a burly gent who had dropped dead of a heart attack a month ago. Rodrigo had never met Sesos—the tapas name for calf brains—before.

Sesos was drinking a glass of *horchata*, a local favorite made from almonds—sweet almond milk. The informant put down the glass and met Rodrigo by a stylized column. "You are searching for the one known as Montalban?"

"His name's Montesa." He produced a photo of the hunted man. "The physical description is as you say. What do you have for me?"

The contact removed his glasses and cleaned them with his handkerchief. Putting them back on, he removed his pipe and said, "He hasn't booked a ticket at the station. A travel agent can arrange it, but your man has not boarded a train here, nor has my associate identified him boarding a ferry to the Balearic Islands."

"So he's still in the city."

"Not necessarily."

Rodrigo checked the time on a large wall clock. Almost six. "I don't have much time, *compadre*. Try not to be too clever, okay? Just give me the short version."

Clearly enjoying his role, Sesos said, "I just got a report of someone vaguely resembling Montalban renting a car near the airport from one of the local low-cost companies."

"Yeah? Now that's good work." Rodrigo opened his wallet, handed over a 200 Euro note, a 50 Euro note and three 20 Euro notes; the large bill was for Sesos, the rest for the local's expenses. "Call me when you've got the name of the rental firm and the make of car with its license number." He held out a business card from Pablo's, a cell number written on back.

Sesos took the card. "Nice doing business with you."

"By the way, what did you do before taking this job?"

The Valencian grinned. "I was a lecturer at the university. In reality, an academic freelancer with no job security."

"Don Miguel takes care of his people."

"So I'd heard."

"By the way, what was your area of expertise?"

"Criminology," Sesos answered and, ignoring a no smoking sign, lit his pipe.

Rodrigo had to laugh.

Chapter 9

S ami and Blackie were no longer under the tree. Anxiously, Rodrigo turned in a circle, looking for them. Couples, young and old, were strolling through the park, enjoying the *paseo*, the traditional evening walk favored by Spaniards. Finally, he saw the van's sliding door half-open and, inside, his dog munching bits of food.

He slid the door fully open. "I forgot to buy dinner."

Sami pressed more food into Blackie's jowls and watched him chomp down on the dry morsels. "A guy with a food cart came by, selling rice and *gambas a la plancha*. The plates are on the counter. Help yourself."

Rodrigo climbed into the van, sat cross-legged by his dog and ate the grilled prawns. "Delicious," he declared. "How's your grub, Blackie?"

The dog kept his own counsel and accepted another small handful of food, followed by pieces of boiled chicken from the fridge.

"So what's the scoop?" she asked.

"Our elusive film star rented a car today. As soon as the make, model and color are confirmed, we'll be able to follow him."

"He can drive anywhere now."

"My guy's watcher will get a fix on the direction."

She petted the dog's head, scratched behind his ears. "I've been thinking."

Rodrigo shoved another tablespoon full of rice into his mouth and chewed slowly. "Thinking is good. What's on your mind?"

"Do you believe in miracles?"

"I'm a Catholic," he confirmed.

She brushed strands of hair from her eyes. "On matters of faith, I don't have much experience. But I try to keep an open mind."

"Exactly what are you getting at?"

"Valencia's cathedral contains the Holy Grail." She leaned back against the under-sink cabinet. "A nun crossing the park explained this while Blackie and I waited. She said many people have been healed in the presence of this relic, which she insisted was the actual cup used by Jesus at the Last Supper.

The agate chalice also caught drops of His Blood at the Crucifixion. Supposedly, Joseph of Arimathea brought the chalice from the Holy Land. Personally, I'm a little skeptical of the authenticity claim, but didn't Jesus say that if you possess faith the size of a mustard seed—one of the smallest of all seeds—you could actually move a mountain?"

Rodrigo put aside the paper plate, wiped his mouth. "You surprise me. A Goth quoting the Bible. Sami, we don't need God's help to find Montesa."

She threw up her hands. "Well, no kidding. I'm talking about your dog!"

"Heal Blackie?"

"Yes. The cathedral tours closed a couple hours ago, but the nun said she'd talk to Padre Phillipe. She was sure he'd give a special dispensation to you and your dog—a private session in the chapel of the Holy Grail. I mean, what have you got to lose?"

Rodrigo touched one of Blackie's paws. The dog thumped his tail. "They'll let a dog in there?"

"Like I said, I've given this some thought and it seems to me there's a reason we're here. No offense, but anyone could catch up with Montesa eventually, right?"

"Wrong. That's why the organization sent me." Rodrigo slid the door closed and climbed into the driver's seat. "We should go to the church now?"

"The priest will be waiting until eight o'clock."

He drove the van the three hundred yards to the cathedral and parked near the bell tower. After putting on his suit jacket, he helped Blackie down and, while Sami locked up, attached a bright orange leash to Blackie's new royal blue collar. The dog kept to the heel position up to a side door of the church. Rodrigo knocked once, softly, and a priest opened.

"Father Phillipe?"

"Come in, come in. So this is the ailing dog." The old priest bent down and let Blackie smell his hand, then rubbed under his chin. "I had a dog like this before I entered the priesthood. Please, follow me."

Sami joined them and closed the door. The church was very old, built in 1262 AD of light-colored stone. The interior smelled of incense, waxed floors, old polished wood, and burning candles.

The priest led them through the main sanctuary, knelt and crossed himself before the ornate altar, and went on to a brick chapel with a simple, unadorned altar holding tall silver candlesticks. Inside a lighted vestibule, elaborately carved images led the viewer's eyes to an illuminated object. There were rows of seats as in any chapel, but the focus was deliberately set on the chalice under the lights.

The dog lay down, exhausted, at the foot of the marble steps below the altar and Rodrigo knelt down and unhooked the leash. "Father, I can never repay you for this kindness. I don't want to cause you any trouble with your superiors. I mean, I gotta answer for my actions too."

The priest spoke educated Spanish in an accent that suggested he was from Galicia, in northwest Spain. "My son," he said softly, "Our Lord is the Creator of all the animals on land, the birds in the sky, the fish in the sea. He placed them on Earth to serve us and, sometimes, to be our companions. We can learn much from them."

"You are a Franciscan?"

The priest nodded. "St. Francis had a special love for God's creatures, wild and domestic, in the air and on the ground. You are now in the presence of a Holy Relic, perhaps the greatest in Christendom.

"Feel free to unburden your heart to Him now." He made the sign of the cross on Blackie's head. "Bless you, loving dog," he said, and left the chapel.

Sami sat in the front row looking, trance-like, from the agate cup to the dog and back to the chalice.

Before the steps of the altar, Rodrigo knelt, crossed himself and placed his rough hands on the sides of Blackie's broad chest.

"God," he began, "I'm not much good at praying. But I gotta help Blackie and I don't know what else to do. Doc Sanchez, he's a good vet," he lowered his voice to a whisper, "but I'm scared of what he's gonna say." He wiped his eyes, patted Blackie a few times. "I can't promise I'll go on a pilgrimage or change a lot..."

He left the leash on the floor of the chapel and slid his arms under Blackie's chest and belly, lifted up the dog and backed away, respectfully, from the shrine.

Sami got the leash and walked behind Rodrigo. They retraced their steps out of the cathedral. She unlocked the van, using the key fob. "That was a beautiful prayer, Rodrigo," she said. "Words from the heart."

"Don't get carried away, girl," he cautioned, and laid the dog on top of the blankets. Suddenly his cell phone rang.

"It might be about the rental."

He answered and listened for a minute. "I'll give Don Miguel a positive report on your work. Good night."

She poured cool water into the dog's dish and watched him lap it up with his large pink tongue. "Got what you need?"

"Spanish-made SEAT four-door sedan. White. We got a license number and his direction—northeast on the AP7, a toll motorway. I'm getting a feel for this guy's moves." He started the motor. "We'll drive out of the city and suburbs and get onto the motorway. After Sagunto, the A23 splits off and runs north to Zaragoza. I think I know where he's travelling to and it's not Barcelona."

"What about stopping to rest? You can't drive all night."

"And risk losing him in the dark? No, we'll pull over at a service station on the A23, sleep for a few hours." Rodrigo peeled off his suit jacket, noticed thick black hair all over the front and the sleeves and balled it up and tossed it toward the back of the van. "Don't shed too much now, old boy. You'll need your fur. The nights are getting cooler."

Sami settled into the passenger seat, a plate of rice and prawns and a bottle of mineral water in her lap. "I'm proud of what you did for Blackie tonight. You took a chance for him, and maybe that's what faith is all about."

He switched on the headlights and pulled away from the cathedral. "You set it up for us, Sami. I owe you. Again."

"Yes, you're deeper in debt now." She forked a prawn into her mouth. "What you prayed...about a pilgrimage? Isn't that exactly what we're doing?"

He snorted. "So young and so wise."

"Okay, driver, let's hit the road," she said, and pointed the tines at the windshield.

Chapter 10

It was dark when Rodrigo suddenly came awake. For a minute he lay still on the carpeted floor of the van, then turned his head and looked at his dog. Blackie was snoring, a reassuring sound to his master. In the dim light cast by the service station's sign into the van, he watched the rise and fall of the dogs chest and tummy and silently gave thanks for another day of life for his loyal Lab.

Then he stretched his arms and legs and, pulling the wool blanket aside, sat up. Once on his feet, he put a pot of water on a burner and lighted the stove and went to the wet bath and shaved and showered. When he came out, Sami was folding the bedding in the back of the van. She looked at him.

"You could have slept in the other bed. I wouldn't have minded."

He nodded. "Your turn in the bath. Make it a 'Navy' shower. Rinse, turn off the hot water, soap down and rinse off. The hot water tank holds only six gallons. By the time you're done, I'll have coffee ready."

After she closed the door to the wet bath compartment, Rodrigo changed clothes. He put on a pair of khakis, a brown T-shirt and, worn outside the belt, a plaid flannel shirt. Then he slipped on his loafers and woke the dog and took Blackie outside to relieve himself.

Back in the van, Rodrigo pulled down the blinds and switched on the LED lights. The water came to a boil on the propane stove and he mixed in coffee powder and creamer. Through the windshield the first reddish streaks appeared in the eastern sky. Time to get going, he thought, and rubbed his neck. "Ready for a car ride, boy?" he asked Blackie, and took a plastic container of chicken from the fridge.

Slowly he fed strips of meat into the dog's mouth and tilted the head back until Blackie had finished chewing and had swallowed the food. He finished with some dry morsels from a bag.

Sami joined them, wearing the same outfit as yesterday. "Clean underwear," she announced, and drank some coffee. "So, what's the plan for today?"

"We're in the Province of Aragon, about 100 miles south of Zaragoza. Then it's decision time. Roads branch east to Barcelona, southeast to Madrid and north to Bilbao."

"You think Montesa will head for the Basque region?"

"Zaragoza has an airport and a train station, but he'll know those are the obvious places we'll have watchers. In addition, some officials are on Don Miguel's Christmas list. I think Senor Montesa will keep driving north. There are car ferries to Portsmouth in the UK out of Bilbao. Also, the Pyrenees are close by. He might figure that our resources are stretched thinner along the French border and he'd be right."

"You've got his plate number. He can't slip through unnoticed."

Rodrigo yawned, set his empty coffee cup in the sink. "Even an amateur can ditch a car in a city's side streets, dispose of the license plates to slow down the search. Someone will accept money to give him a lift—maybe a truck driver. In which case, he just might slip through since our influence with immigration and customs isn't so great up there."

She took out her phone. "Come on, Ruben, wake up." Finally, her associate answered and gave her the tip she needed. She put down the phone. "There's a girl in Zaragoza. She's got some information for us."

Rodrigo started the diesel engine and pulled onto the motorway just as the sun came up over the hills of eastern Aragon. "We'll be there by mid-morning. Call her and tell her to wait in the Plaza del Pilar."

The drive was uneventful and he kept to the legal limit, 75 mph. While steering, he munched on a buttered roll and drank more coffee that Sami had made. She sat beside the dog, stroking his fur and whispering.

"Hey," he said, "you might be interested to know that your ancestors once ruled this region."

"My mother can trace her lineage back hundreds of years to the Moors."

"That's not what I meant. The Visigoths, barbarians from northern Europe, invaded the Iberian Peninsula after the fall of the Roman Empire during the 5th century. They converted to Christianity. Some of their churches, castles and buildings remain. But they were no match for the Moors in 711. Those guys were unstoppable until the Frankish army of Charles Martel turned them back from France."

"Jamie said you were well-read. However, for your information, the Visigoths have no connection to Goth people today. It's more of a lifestyle statement."

"And fashion." Rodrigo glanced at Blackie. "Not that I'm complaining. I like black."

Much of Zaragoza had been destroyed during Spain's Civil War in 1936-1939, with some of the bitterest fighting between Franco's Nationalist forces and the Republican army occurring in Aragon province. The city had been rebuilt, with some structures like the Basilica de Nuestra Senora del Pilar left intact. The cathedral was topped with eleven tile-roofed cupolas, a distinctive architectural style that conveyed an Italian influence.

Standing by the front of the church, Sami's informant was unmistakable in a long black skirt, pink blouse and, most striking of all, an untamed head of orange-tinted hair. The source put out her cigarette and approached the van.

"Get in the passenger seat," Sami instructed, and made the introductions. "Rodrigo, this is Carmen."

He stared at the wolf's head tattoo on the left side of her neck, then at her pierced lower lip. "Carmen who?"

The orange-haired girl said in a raw, smoker's voice, "Carmen. That's all you need to know."

Rodrigo shook his head. "I need to know a lot more than that, sweetheart. What is your name and where are you from?"

Carmen made a face, looked back at Sami. "Is this guy for real?"

Blackie let loose a low growl and Sami said, "Better tell him what he wants to know."

She licked her lips, stared straight ahead. "Carmen Brown, Manchester."

"What's an English girl doing in Zaragoza?"

"Son-of-a—"

"Don't say it," Rodrigo cautioned.

"Say what? I mean, what the—"

"No profanity."

Carmen's eyes looked at Rodrigo, her green eyes glowing. "Are you crazy or some kind of priest? You don't look like a priest."

Sami said, "In this van, no cussing, no swearing, no taking God's name in vain. Those are the rules."

"I'll bet you look at me and think I'm weird," the English girl said, "but let me tell you, *you* guys are *very* strange. What's the deal here? Are you escapees from a monastery?"

"His dog is ill. Everyone knows that it's best to maintain a positive attitude when faced with something like cancer. You following me, Carmen?"

She started to light a cigarette, glanced at Rodrigo—who shook his head—and put the cigarette back in the pack. "I'll try to understand."

"Vulgar language draws upon negative energy," Sami explained, "so we keep it clean. Also, cussing demonstrates a lack of control over your words. If you can't tame your tongue, you're of little use to us."

Carmen blinked, looked back at Blackie. "Sorry, dog, I want you to get better. I really do."

"Good enough," Rodrigo said, put the van in drive gear and drove out of the plaza and onto a bridge over the Ebro River. "Did you see the one I'm after?"

"We're talking about the guy from the *Fantasy Island*? My mother loved the show...watched the original episodes and every rerun on the telly."

"That's him, the Montalban double. Which way did he go?" The turnoff to Barcelona loomed ahead.

"He drove north in a white sedan, took the A68 in the direction of the Basque country." Her hand rested on the door handle. "You can let me out here."

"Not yet, Carmen. Buckle your seat belt," Rodrigo ordered. "You're coming with us."

Chapter 11

The forested hills and fertile farming valleys of the southern Basque region featured vineyards and golden fields of wheat, with small villages and towns which they passed over quickly on the motorway north to Bilbao.

The Basque separatist movement had not disappeared entirely, though presently it was not as active as in the recent past. The Basques were an ancient people of unknown origin, not ethnically related to other residents of the Iberian Peninsula.

Rodrigo stopped once for diesel fuel and to let Blackie move about on a stretch of green grass. About three hours out of Zaragoza the motorway cut through the barren hills above Bilbao, a largely industrial city set on the banks of the River Nervion, which emptied into an estuary on the Bay of Biscay.

Rodrigo drove down a city street toward the ultra-modern Guggenheim Museum and found a convenient parking spot.

"What are we doing here?" Sami asked.

"Our quarry likes to trade on his appearance by mingling with tourists. He's probably looking for an easy mark, a middle-aged woman alone on holiday. Then he'll sweet talk her into giving him a ride across the border."

"Or onto a ferry to Portsmouth," Sami said and gazed toward the water.

"Too confined. Once on, he's trapped. And with a face like his, he *will* be recognized." Rodrigo opened the driver's door. "Since I'm the most normal-looking in our trio, I'll check around, ask some questions of the museum staff."

Carmen started to say something, then closed her mouth and began chewing on her fluorescent-orange painted fingernails.

Sami lowered a bowl of water for Blackie, but the dog refused to drink. "I'm taking Blackie outside for some air," she told Rodrigo. From the sidewalk, the dog limped to a 43-foot tall terrier sculpture covered with a coat of flowers, a favorite statue of the locals. He tried to pee without success, something that had become more and more common.

"It's okay, boy. Don't worry about it," she said. "Just try to drink more water. No water, no pee."

"Maybe he's got a UTI," Carmen observed. "He feels an urgency to urinate but nothing happens. See, I was a nurse in the UK." She lit a cigarette. "The internal plumbing isn't all that different, just more horizontal in dogs."

She looked down at the dog and quickly put out the cigarette. "I can see your friend, Rodrigo, is pretty sensitive about his dog's condition, so I wouldn't tell him this. If the dog has cancer, it may've spread to the kidneys or bladder and that's what's causing the irritation he's feeling."

Sami hugged the Labrador retriever and helped him sit down—a change in position that had become an awkward affair, since the hind legs were losing strength and, presumably, coordination. "What you doing in Spain, Carmen?"

"Looking for a husband, what else?" She cut short a laugh.

"Can I give you a piece of advice?"

"I'm 25. My Mum married at 17. She thinks I'm a hopeless case. Maybe I am. Anyway, I needed a break from hospital work, so I'm on tour. Two months in Spain and, in another month I'm off to Italy." She shrugged. "Yeah sure, Samantha, go ahead and advise."

"Have you looked in a mirror lately? Okay, maybe I don't look like the marrying kind either. Or perhaps I'm still young enough to dream that everything will turn out all right."

She kissed the top of Blackie's head. "Who do you think will be attracted to you except some mixed-up guy, Carmen?" She held up a hand. "I know that's a harsh assessment, but sometimes I stare into a mirror and think, 'no good man is going to fall for me.'"

"That *is* a little cold-blooded." With her tongue, Carmen felt the stainless ball jutting from her lip. "Tell you what, I'll think about it."

Sami smiled. "Let's get Blackie back to the van."

"Wait a minute. Surely you've noticed your friend's resemblance to a young Charles Bronson in *The Magnificent Seven*? If he watches Bronson's early '70s movies like *Telefon, St. Ives,* and the one where he played a watermelon farmer in Colorado, *Mr. Majestyk,* Rodrigo will be able to see what he'll look like in a few years. It's remarkable, don't you think?"

"You've watched all of his old films?"

"My Mum had a crush on Stone Face. She played his films over and over on her VCR."

"Women," Sami laughed, "aren't we something?"

The aroma of grilled lamb filled the van as Rodrigo climbed in, carrying paper plates of the freshly-cooked meat. He passed them to his companions and set his on the counter. After rubbing his dog, he looked up. "A museum guide recalled seeing Montesa before noon—thought he was a genuine body double for the *Fantasy Island* star. Said he strolled out of the museum in the company of a well-dressed woman and suggested that I speak with a nearby car park attendant. Montesa's vehicle is still on the street. He left in the woman's car which, from its markings, the attendant guessed was a rental."

"Which way did they go?" Sami asked.

"Hard to tell from this location." He grabbed his plate and started eating. Between mouthfuls he said, "Our eyes on the ferry dock reported that he hasn't seen the guy today, so we'll travel east toward San Sebastian which is only a few miles from the French border.

"In late September, the city has a big film festival that draws hundreds of thousands. If today's pickup doesn't work out, he might stick around until the crowds arrive for the film fest, lose himself in the masses of people and take advantage of his TV star looks and charm to entice another female to drive him over the Pyrenees."

The fifty miles on the AP8 toll motorway flew by and they were soon at the seaside resort city of San Sebastian. Rodrigo drove to the eastern edge of town and stopped at a service station to ask questions of the cashier.

Back at the van he said, "We caught a break. A lady, speaking Spanish with a German accent, filled her tank here and continued east toward the border. The cashier noted that the man beside her was a dead ringer for Montalban."

"What if they cross over before we get there?" Carmen asked.

"Then he wins." Rodrigo winked at Sami. "But I'm wagering he's still in Spanish territory. At midday in my country, things move at a leisurely pace."

Sure enough, several miles ahead the cars were bunched up in a long queue. Rodrigo pulled onto the shoulder and got down. "I'm going for a walk. See if Blackie will eat a few bites, okay?"

He strolled along the shoulder, ignoring buses and trucks, glancing into car windows. Less than a mile from the van he found what he was looking for and tapped on the passenger-side's glass. The occupant, reluctantly, lowered the window. One look at the man's features told him the hunt was over. He reached in, unlocked the door and opened it.

"Senor Montesa, my name is Rodrigo. Rodrigo of Seville, if you know what I mean?"

Montesa sighed and, as his female companion started to protest, told her, "It is all right, Frau Kohl. You have been most kind. I must leave you now but, rest assured, I will be in touch with you soon." The film star look-alike got out of the car, unlocked the back door and removed a single carry-on piece of hard luggage, extended the handle and walked up the road beside Rodrigo.

"How did you find me?"

Rodrigo spread out his hands. "Fortunately for me, you have a face no one can forget."

From the van, Rodrigo called Juan Barquero, who agreed to send an escort to the Zaragoza airport to accompany Senor Montesa back to Seville. With that, Rodrigo led Montesa to the table at the back of the van and tied his hands and feet with twine. Blackie growled at the new passenger for a couple of minutes, then lay back down.

"As a gentleman, I should not have to secure you like this. Your word not to run again should be enough, but...you know how it is."

"What will happen to me?" Montesa asked.

"You will find the money to repay Don Miguel. Then Senor Garcia will be happy, and you will be free to go wherever you like. Even Germany."

Rodrigo started the van and turned it westward toward San Sebastian and Bilbao. "I will drop you off," he told Carmen, "where we met."

"If you don't mind," she said, keeping her hands on her lap, "I'd like to go to Seville. Can I travel there with you?"

Rodrigo smiled. "Since you ask so nicely," he glanced back at Sami, "how can I refuse?"

Chapter 12

" Put your dog on the walk-on scale," the pretty assistant said. "Hold him steady."

Doctor Sanchez insisted on a clean animal hospital. Rodrigo's nose twitched at the smell of antiseptics and cleaning solutions as he pulled Blackie closer and, with an upward tug on his collar, got him onto the scale. Seeing how much muscle and fat the dog had lost brought a lump to his throat. He'd noticed the progressive loss of muscle mass while on the road, but had tried not to think too much about it, fearful of what it meant.

The scale's LED readout put the dog's weight at 59 pounds, a loss of six since the last visit.

The young woman led them to an exam room and took vital signs, which the dog didn't seem to mind until she slid a thermometer into his back passage. Rodrigo held Blackie still during that uncomfortable procedure.

Afterward, while Rodrigo sat on a chair murmuring words of reassurance, she typed the results into the computer. A minute later, Doc Sanchez entered the room, greeted his patients and then silently observed Blackie from a couple of feet away. Finally the vet knelt down and ran his experienced hands over the animal, paying special attention to the hind legs. Blackie grew tired of trying to gain purchase on the slippery linoleum—his nails were sliding on the floor. Awkwardly he lowered himself and stretched out his forelegs.

Doc Sanchez stood up slowly and leaned against the counter. "He doesn't look good, Rodrigo. Not good at all."

"You don't pull any punches, Doc."

"I was afraid of this." The vet checked the weight figures of the past two and a half weeks. His gray eyes went back to the dog. "It could be osteomyelitis or a fungal infection. But the most likely cause...well, I'd like to take a chest x-ray and another picture of that leg." He turned to the assistant. "The leg first. If it's what I suspect, we don't need one of the chest, too. No need to sedate him."

Rodrigo walked his dog to the back room where the machine was located. As he helped lift Blackie onto the table, he told the technician, "The doc said to check the leg first, then the chest."

The tech, a tall blond girl, stiffened. "Sir, I know my job."

Rodrigo nodded and returned to the exam room to wait. All kinds of thoughts erupted in his brain. He held his head in his hands. Sami had wanted to come to the clinic with them, but he'd told her to stay at the cottage and get things ready for the next trip. Now he wished that she was here. Maybe she would've said something encouraging. Still, that wouldn't've changed Blackie's condition.

The old vet came back to the room, hands in the pockets of his white lab coat. He looked down at the floor as the assistant brought the dog in. Then he looked Rodrigo in the eye and said, "Nothing can be done."

"What do you mean?" Rodrigo blurted.

"I mean, there's nothing I can do for him."

"You spoke of surgery."

"He doesn't look good at all," the vet repeated and sighed.

Stunned, Rodrigo said, "There must be *something*."

"Amputation is the usual answer. If I take off the leg, he will live another two months...maybe a little longer. At Blackie's age, anesthesia and surgery are especially difficult for the animal."

"I've seen dogs walk on three legs."

"They bear more weight on the forelegs. But with the strain of an operation and recovery...I'm afraid it won't buy much extra time."

"What about chemotherapy?"

Doc Sanchez shook his head. "I won't offer you false hope. By mistake, the tech went ahead and took the chest x-ray. There are spots on his lungs. Honestly, Rodrigo, by the time this type of cancer is diagnosed, it has usually spread from the bone to the lungs. Like I said, nothing can be done."

"Nothing?"

"Most people have their pet put down."

Rodrigo clipped the leash on his dog and got up. "I'll take him home. Can you give something for pain?"

"Of course," the vet said, and wrote out a prescription.

Chapter 13

"I'm coming with you," Sami insisted. "You need my help, tracking down the Fat One."

"Stay with Blackie. He needs you more."

"We got the TV star's double together. We can do it again."

"Not this time."

"*My* contacts led us to Montesa as much as yours."

Rodrigo kicked at the dry dirt in front of his cottage. "Yeah, you've got a point."

"Then let's pack up and go get this guy." The dog hobbled up to her side. "Ready for another van ride?"

It didn't take long to finish making preparations for the journey. As for the suspect, the last sighting of him was on the A66 motorway, headed north through the Sierra Morena mountains, possibly trying to cross the border into Portugal.

With Rodrigo's mind preoccupied, Sami was determined to be there for him with any of the resources at her disposal which, as in Morocco, consisted mainly of the young, restless and underemployed.

Many of these undervalued citizens were very creative in their means of support—talents that their societies could've put to better use if public policy mandated it and private business exercised more imagination. The percentage of jobless youth in Spain rivaled that of Morocco, hence many were studying German in an effort to enhance their prospects of landing a paying position in the economic powerhouse of Europe.

"What's our destination?" she asked.

"Salamanca."

She studied his paper map of the country. "In the province of Castilla y Leon. We're passing through the Extremadura, altogether over 250 miles, to gather background on El Gordo?"

"I never went to a university. One thing I've learned about college boys is that they always remember their time at university as the glory years. Senor Jaca will leave clues to his escape route by returning to a place he considers safe and memorable. After that, he'll make his move for the border. And that border runs for hundreds of miles along Castilla y Leon and south along the western edge of the Extremadura and into Andalusia. We've gotta get a fix on his likeliest exit point from Spain." Rodrigo looked over his shoulder at his dog. "Has he eaten anything today?"

"Some dry food, practically forced on him."

"Water?"

"He drank a little from the garden hose before leaving."

"I can't afford to waste time nailing El Gordo. I gotta feeling Blanco's gonna be the hardest and I want my dog home when," Rodrigo coughed, "you know...when the time comes."

"He doesn't act like he's in pain."

"Doc gave some pills."

"Tylenol 4. That's strong stuff. Sure you want to give to your dog?"

"I read that bone cancer can hurt almost as bad as stomach cancer, but what do I know? For now, we give him what he's taken in the past."

"Where'd you learn that trick, putting the pill in butter?"

"Doc told me."

"Don't give up, Rodrigo. God heard your prayer in Valencia, I know He did."

"Spiritual comfort from a Goth?"

She looked out the window, said nothing more.

By early afternoon they had passed through Spain's old western frontier province, an expanse of green, rock-strewn hills and forest lands lush with wild game. The cities and towns reflected a turbulent past, when Christians and Moors battled for the country, and military-type monastic orders built strong-walled monasteries where monks helped defend the region for the king. Many of the towns retained their medieval walls and, going back even farther in time, stone bridges built by the Romans remained in use over many of the rivers.

The motorway cut through the center of the province and, in the early afternoon, they arrived in the southern Castilla y Leon city of Salamanca. They drove across the Puente Romano, not surprisingly, a stone bridge constructed in the 1st century by Roman engineers. The city's oldest quarter was set on a hill straight head, with a double cathedral—so-called because it consisted of two churches, the *Catedral Vieja* and the *Catedral Nueva,* the former a Romanesque cathedral, the latter mainly Gothic—towering, into the blue sky, commanding attention.

But it was Salamanca's 13th century university, the country's oldest and, some maintained, finest, that interested Rodrigo and he found a place to park just outside the old city center. Leaving Sami and his dog in the van, he walked to the university and randomly struck up conversations with students, showing a photo of Pedro Jaca and gauging their reaction. After an hour, a pre-med student—he could tell by the textbooks—agreed that a man matching El Gordo's description had, indeed, been in the area yesterday.

"Did you see where he went?" Rodrigo asked.

"Yes. In fact, I saw him twice."

"Yesterday?"

"That's what I said," the spectacled student answered impatiently. "The odd thing is that, when he walked through the plaza in the morning, he looked like the one in the photo except that he had a heavy, three day beard. He was headed up the Calle de San Pablo toward the Plaza Mayor." The young man shifted his books from his left arm to the right. "Then, in the late afternoon, as I was leaving a lab class, he reappeared. Only he was different."

"You're sure it was the same guy?"

"I've studied anatomy and physiology. Someday I hope to practice cosmetic surgery."

"Smart. Very smart," Rodrigo said, and grinned. "So, how did he look?"

"Still overweight, but he'd shaved his head. He was completely bald, with that fur ball around the mouth so many American tourist guys wear." The serious student had to laugh. "It was the Hawaiian shirt that really caught my eye, made me look closer. Definitely, it was the guy in your picture."

"Any bookstores on the street to the Plaza Mayor?"

"This *is* a university town."

"You're pretty sharp, kid. Maybe I should call you Doc?"

"Miguel is fine."

"Tell you what, you ever decide to practice in Seville, or anywhere in Andalusia, you ask around for another Miguel—Don Miguel—and I'll vouch for you."

Chapter 14

A small brass bell rang as he entered the ground floor of a bookstore across from the Plaza del Corrillo. Wooden shelves full of hardcover books soared over his head, some accessible only by a rolling ladder.

Tables piled with books occupied the center of the store. Rodrigo loved to read and felt right at home. He also felt a bit guilty to enjoy the place while his dog lay ill in the van, so he approached a clerk and produced the photo of Jaca.

"Ever seen this guy?"

The clerk, a nervous older woman, moved back a step. "Why do you want to know?"

"There is an old debt to repay."

"You owe him money or he owes you?"

"It's complicated." Thinking of Blackie, he didn't want to lie.

The clerk adjusted the glasses on her nose and, taking the photo, peered at it for a full minute. "Yes, he was here," she said, and handed it back. "He didn't buy any books."

"Did he buy anything?"

"Senor, this is a bookshop."

Feeling rebuked, Rodrigo pocketed the picture. "Thank you for your time, Senora." He looked around the store. "I like this place a lot. It's got that literary kind of atmosphere...a real class place."

Suddenly the clerk softened. "He bought a map," she volunteered.

"A map? Do you recall what it covered?"

She took the ballpoint pen clipped to her starched blouse and tapped it on her front teeth. "It was a map of the Extremadura province. He said he was a birdwatcher."

"Gracias, Senora." He took the hand without the pen and kissed it. "I will remember your kindness."

She blushed. "Please, feel free to come back."

On the street nearest the university he saw a barber shop and entered, photo in hand. Yes, the elderly barber told him, he had used his trusty straight razor to clear the hair from the man's head, as well as to carve out the desired facial hair. The man had paid cash, had even added a substantial tip. Oddly, he had taken a bright yellow shirt with red flowers out of a plastic shopping bag and had replaced his plain shirt with it, claiming that a haircut always made his neck itch, getting into the collar and so on. Rodrigo thanked the talkative barber and returned to the van.

On the way out of the city Rodrigo stopped at a small restaurant. "Since we're close to Extremadura, ask for bowls to go of *gazpacho manchego*. I'll take Blackie out for a walk."

The dog on his blankets in the van, eating small pieces of chicken when she climbed back inside, carrying a ceramic pot. "They don't have containers for takeout. We'll empty the stew into our own pot and return this." As she transferred the thick stew, the scent of wild game stimulated the dog's sense of smell and he ate more food from Rodrigo's hand. "It's partridge and wild rabbit meat. What a treat!"

"Enjoy it, Sami. It may also serve as an early dinner. I'm not sure of the services where we're going."

After eating, they retraced their route, taking the same motorway roughly 80 miles south to Plasencia, a walled city on the banks of the River Jerte. A short stop for diesel and they drove south on a paved secondary road to Villareal de San Carlos, a small town on the edge of the Park of Monfrague, a nature reserve. The surrounding land was dotted with cork oak and holm oak—trees common to Morocco—making it familiar scenery to Sami. There were also scrubby hillsides and rocky crags in the park, home to many of the species of the country's migratory birds, particularly during the month of September.

Sightings of black storks and black vultures, in particular, were highly-sought by birdwatchers from around the world, dedicated men and women who willingly made the trek to this remote, protected park. As a bonus, the truly fortunate might catch a fleeting glimpse of the rare lynx, among other mammals.

Rodrigo had explained to Sami his discoveries in the streets and shops of Salamanca. "Once again, I must ask that you stay by the van for Blackie while I scout around. I doubt that El Gordo has remained here. Still, in his loud outfit someone will remember seeing him."

"You really think he'd make a detour to such a remote place?"

"I think he is waiting for someone...before making his move for Portugal. In the meantime, he probably hopes that his over-the-top disguise will have transformed him into just another middle-aged guy from the USA, desperately trying to avoid the curse of male pattern baldness."

"That wouldn't be so sad if those guys looked like Yul Brynner. Instead most of them come across like Telly Savalas in Kojak," she grimaced, "round bowling ball heads and overweight."

"Most of America's current crop of macho boys have never heard of those actors. In Europe, Americans are known for their short memories and limited attention spans." He rummaged through a cabinet and brought out a pair of Zeiss binoculars. "Essential for any serious birdwatcher," he said, and petted his dog. "Bye, Blackie. Listen to Sami and drink some water."

He hiked into the park for a couple of miles, pausing now and then to train his binoculars on birds in the air, some catching updrafts and soaring high above the cliffs. Using a guide booklet he'd picked up at the information center, he identified a black-winged kite and, feeling proud of his observation skills, almost bumped into a casually-dressed couple, also using binoculars.

"Excuse me," he said.

"It's okay, senor," the fortyish man said in a New England accent. "My wife and I just saw a stork beyond the olive trees, around the bend in this path."

"Can I ask how long you've been here?"

"We came yesterday morning. We're staying in Plasencia."

"Did you come across a big guy, maybe wearing a bright tropical shirt."

"Bald?"

"That's him."

"He was here today. Saw him near the information center at noon, getting into a car."

"Do you recall which way he went?"

The American looked to his wife. She said, "South, across the river. Is he a friend of yours?"

"Not exactly. Thank you and good luck spotting an Imperial eagle."

"You saw one here?" the man asked excitedly.

"Not today. But I hope *you* spot one." Rodrigo had to admit that either luck or God was on his side. In addition, he'd have to revise his opinion of American men nowadays. Not all of them had fallen from grace since he had departed Brooklyn.

Chapter 15

The river was wide—it was now part of a reservoir. The American woman had pointed them in the right direction and they followed the two lane blacktop into an increasingly rugged landscape, the air cooler as they climbed higher into the hill country. Sami found a shawl in a wardrobe and wrapped it around her shoulders. For Rodrigo, a short leather jacket sufficed. Blackie enjoyed his master's wool blanket, draped over him up to his neck.

By dinnertime they had reached the hilltop town of Trujillo. Rodrigo made the decision to pass the night there. He found a spot off the road next to some wild olive trees and switched off the ignition.

"What if the police stop to question why we're not in an official campsite?"

"Before it is dark I will pop open the hood and remove a part, disabling the vehicle. When it doesn't start up, they will understand."

"The town isn't far. Want me to walk up there and buy some food?"

"I have heard that it is very beautiful in the evening when the Plaza Mayor is floodlit. There are highly-regarded restaurants on the square so, yes, bring back some lamb stew. If necessary, you can buy a ceramic bowl at a shop." He handed her small denomination bills.

"Trujillo has quite a history. Many of the conquistadors are from this area, the Pizarro brothers especially. Francisco Pizarro made a name for himself, defeating the Incas of Peru with only a small force of men on horseback. After destroying an ancient people's empire he married an Incan woman and brought her back to this place. Personally, I consider the Pizarro family a bunch of butchers."

"You are a good man, Rodrigo."

"I am not one of God's favorites."

"Oh, I don't know about that."

"It is true. I am one of God's losers."

"So were most of his disciples," she countered, and opened the passenger door and slid off the seat. "After dinner don't expect any water to flow from the tap of the sink. I've got to wash my hair and that means I'm using all the water in the freshwater tank. It's the price you pay when you bring a woman along."

In the fading light he watched her trudge up the road as the town center lit up, bathing part of Trujillo in a soft glow. Getting out of the driver's seat, he went to Blackie, lifted him up and took him outside to sniff around and take care of business. Thankfully, the dog still had enough strength in his back muscles and hind legs to squat. Blackie had pride and obviously wanted to take care of its own basic needs—that is, except for eating.

Running low on chicken, perhaps he will try the lamb, Rodrigo thought, and remembered the vet's comment before leaving the clinic—echoing what Sami had started to say in Valencia—that animals know when they are seriously ill.

If badly injured, they go into shock, blunting the pain and easing their suffering. If they are very sick and unlikely to recover, an animal senses it and withdraws from its natural hunger for food—much as a terminally ill person in hospice grows resigned to the end and, gradually denied fluids, expires from severe dehydration—supposedly a relatively painless death.

Rodrigo looked up to the sky, as if searching for God's place in Heaven, and sighed heavily. "Thank you, Lord," he said aloud, "for this dog's life. He is Your creature. You loaned him to me to share my life. I gotta say I'm grateful for the years together. It's just that it is so hard to think of losing him..." Then he choked up and, holding his dog close, picked him up and went back inside the van.

"I love you, boy," he said, and rubbed the dog's chest and legs, felt the large paws and nails, and tried to smile. The Lab's big brown eyes were now a bit sunken in their sockets and the top of his head was becoming even more sharply defined, the typical broad flatness gone.

"You're a good dog," he said, and kissed Blackie's head. "The best."

Chapter 16

The road to the small city of Guadalupe wove through the Sierra de Guadalupe along ridges, lots of twists and turns in the narrow ribbon of blacktop until they reached the Sierra de Villuercas range, a journey that would have been exciting in a sports car, but was more of a chore in a high-roofed van.

Coming around a bend in the road, the early morning sun shone off the tall stone walls of the Monasterio de Guadalupe, a fortress-like structure that dominated a town of whitewashed buildings and red tile roofs. The monastery dated from the year 1340 and featured square battlements as well as round turreted towers, lending it the aura of a castle.

With the influx of wealth from the New World in the 15th and 16th centuries, the monastery had grown into a famous center of learning, hosting schools of medicine and pharmacy, as well as a hospital. But those years of renown had ended abruptly with the arrival of Napoleon's French army.

Nowadays, the cloister housed Franciscan monks, while other Gothic-styled buildings contained museums for embroidery, sculpture and paintings. The church was a destination for Roman Catholic pilgrims, with the Virgin of Guadalupe the main object of veneration.

Allegedly found by a shepherd in a nearby hillside in the early 1300s, the wooden statue was dressed in formal robes, the faces of the mother of Jesus and the Christ child on her lap blackened over the centuries by smoke from lamps in the church. Pilgrims passed behind the altar to touch her dress and, perhaps, receive an answer to prayer—for prosperity, for happiness, for healing from some affliction...whatever burden their souls carried.

At the monastery's car park, Sami got down from the van, still wearing her black clothing (she had washed her underclothes in the shower and air dried them). She snugged the wool shawl around her shoulders to ward off the morning chill. "Are you thinking what I'm thinking?"

"I don't know," Rodrigo confessed.

"We take Blackie into the church, brush his coat against the Virgin's dress."

"You've done your homework on this place. But no, I don't think we should do that."

"I thought most Spanish guys venerated the Mother of Christ like she's the Queen of Heaven."

"What you say is largely true, even by those who are not devout Catholics."

"Some have suggested that the practice goes back to the ancient world's agricultural-based worship of a fertility goddess," she pointed out.

"Perhaps that is still the way for a few. Others see the Virgin Mary sitting at Christ's right hand as someone more approachable than the Lord—like their own mother—a lady, not a god, who might understand their prayers and intercede for them. As for me, I honor her as the greatest woman who ever lived."

He finished a cup of coffee, now cold. "Imagine her life, the way people in Nazareth must've talked when she was pregnant and unmarried. She knew what had happened—God sent the Archangel Gabriel to explain it—but, even in those days, how many believed in the truth of dreams and visions? And Joseph, he was a stand-up guy, a real man, marrying her in spite of rumors flying around town. Mary, Mother of God, is someone worthy of honor and respect, but I don't worship her and I won't ask her to heal my dog. Only God can do that, if He wants to."

"How can she be the Mother of God?"

"She was the mother of Jesus, Son of God, when He became a man on Earth. You know, God the Father, God the Son, God the Holy Spirit...one God in three persons." Rodrigo shrugged. "Look, I'm not educated. I can't explain the nature of God. I'm not a priest or theologian. In any case, why should we expect to understand everything about God? That'd be pretty arrogant."

"I can agree with that," she said, and gestured at the walled monastery. "What are the chances El Gordo is in there now?"

"Pretty good. After years of tracking down guys, I can tell." He pointed at the car beside her. "A rental car."

"Lots of pilgrims travel to this place," she reminded him. "Look at all the tour buses in the car park."

"Most tourists don't leave binoculars and Hawaiian shirts lying on the back seat of their car."

She looked through the car's side windows. "You *are* good at this. Let's go get this dirtbag."

"Blackie?"

"Okay," she nodded, "I'll wait here for you."

Inside the monastery, Rodrigo quickly recognized the Fat One inside the museum devoted to hand-illustrated and colored manuscripts, each one painstakingly produced and copied by monks during the medieval period before the invention of movable type by a German, Johannes Gutenberg.

The big guy wore a dark red wool sweater; otherwise, his clean shaven head gleamed under the lights. While the guide explained the process of creating the manuscripts, Pedro Jaca kept glancing at his wristwatch. Rodrigo's assumption that Jaca was killing time before making his move toward Portugal looked more and more plausible. Probably planning to meet someone here, leave the rented vehicle behind to confuse any pursuers, he decided, and drive across the border as a passenger—like Montesa had tried. The other possibility was that Jaca would join one of the tour groups and travel with them.

As the guide led the visitors over to the museum of embroidery, Rodrigo cut in front of a middle-aged couple and bumped into El Gordo. "You should come with me, Senor Jaca," he said quietly, in Spanish.

The Fat One looked at Rodrigo, blinked his eyes several times and, perhaps, while considering his options, stepped aside from the group. "I was close to getting away. What led you here?"

In the open courtyard, Rodrigo faced the fugitive. "*You* led me here. You, a Spaniard, tried to be someone else...an American. A man should always be content to be himself."

"Is Senor Garcia angry?"

Rodrigo shook his head. "It's just business."

"My wife's cousin drives a tour bus out of Lisbon. He was going to take me through the border."

"I figured it was something like that. Well, the only airport in this province is in Badajoz, only miles from Portugal—as close as you're going to get, I'm afraid. I'll drive you there."

"You'll let me fly back to Seville alone?"

"Don Miguel will send an escort."

"You drove here?"

"You got that right."

"I don't mind riding back to Seville with you. I won't try to escape. Not again."

"Sorry, a man of your size...it's the close quarters." He rubbed his neck, working out the tension. "And my dog wouldn't like it."

"A dog?" El Gordo started to perspire, and wiped his face with a dirty handkerchief. "I am scared of dogs."

"Tell you what, since you're so cooperative now, I'll let you sit up front with me. Just don't try to jump out while we're moving."

Staring down at the flagstones, Jaca nodded over and over. "My running days are over."

Chapter 17

Backtracking from Badajoz to Salamanca brought them, once again, to the medieval city in the late afternoon. Rodrigo pulled into a service station and cut the motor. Stepping out of the red van he made a call and, after refueling, got back in. He cupped Blackie's head in his hands. "How you doin', old boy? Think you can make one more trip before going home?"

The dog's brown eyes focused intently on his master; loyalty and affection shone through.

"Here's the deal," he told Sami. "Blanco was ID'd by one of our guys in Vigo, a city on the northwest coast of Galicia. Vigo is Spain's largest fishing port. Jorge Blanco was asking around about shipping out as a paying passenger on one of the larger trawlers, one headed across the North Atlantic to fish the waters near Canada. Galician fleets still catch off our coast, but overfishing has become a problem so some of the bigger vessels cross the ocean."

"A fishing boat's captain would take that chance with a guy like Blanco?" Sami asked. "It's not like he could pass for a member of the crew."

"Taking a passenger along on a working boat is rarely done, not like with freighters carrying a few travellers for extra money. But for enough cash, who knows? Anyway, word of a stranger gets around in port and my guy picked up on it."

"How far is it?"

"Just north of Portugal. We'll drive on through Zamora, turn west for Puebla de Sanabria and spend the night there. I'd like to push on to

Vigo but," he lowered his voice to a whisper, "my friend isn't getting any stronger."

"At least we're able to help him walk."

"Your idea of using a bath towel like a sling under his belly has made a big difference."

Sami rose from the floor by the dog and gripped Rodrigo's left arm. "You've got to keep faith."

"Sure. But what do you think is gonna happen?"

She sighed. "I'm hoping for a miracle...and I'm not even much of a believer."

"I want to catch this Blanco guy and get back home before the end. You know what I mean?"

She held up a towel that she'd placed under his belly. "Blood mixed with urine. He hadn't been going much since we left Seville. Now it's too much. Losing blood'll leave him weaker. While we're in Salamanca we should stop at a supermarket and buy some incontinent pads. They're absorbent so the fluid won't ruin his bedding, and less moisture will cling to his coat and skin."

Has the cancer reached his bladder? Rodrigo wondered. He scratched behind his dog's ears, ruffled its chest fur. "Hang on, Blackie, we'll be home soon."

While Sami sat down by the dog and tilted a soft plastic squeeze bottle of water into his mouth, Rodrigo started up the van and drove back onto the highway. On the northern outskirts of the city he saw a store and pulled into the parking lot.

Sami got out and declined the cash he offered. "I've got money. Let me do this for Blackie."

"Get broth."

"Broth? You mean bouillon cubes?"

"Cans of chicken broth."

She entered the store and bought pads for the dog, three cans of broth and, for themselves, some fruit—local cherries—Iberian ham and a loaf of bread. Leaving the motorway at Zamora, they followed a highway northwest until it connected with the A52, the motorway into the Province of Galicia. Before dark they reached the lake resort area of Puebla de Sanabria. Rodrigo carried the dog out. He held a bath towel under Blackie's tummy, a support for the dog's weak, nearly uncoordinated hind legs so that the animal could get some exercise. Even when Blackie had been able to walk without assistance, a couple of days ago, he had stumbled and fallen back onto his rump several times and had struggled to get up again.

Now a tendency to walk more diagonally than straight was becoming more pronounced. It was obvious that the dog was trying its best to please his master, even trying to eat some food though it, apparently, had lost the taste or desire to eat. For a meal that evening, Rodrigo filled the plastic bottle with lukewarm broth and Blackie drank it from the spout inserted into his mouth. Afterward, the dog appeared more alert.

"Sodium helps," Rodrigo explained to Sami. "With the recent loss of fluid, I'm worried about his electrolytes getting out of balance. Short of getting blood work done, I don't really know what's going on, but he's probably losing potassium. Calcium, too. That can affect muscle strength and coordination. Also, the broth's gotta have some protein, vitamins and minerals. Good stuff."

"How do you know these things?"

"Boxing. Full workouts in the gym, road work—running distances—means sweating a lot, especially in our climate. Without replacing fluids and minerals a fighter'd weaken and faint." He rinsed out the bottle in the sink. "Actually, I'm guessing at some of this. Short of an IV, broth is all I can think of."

The only indication the dog gave of pain came after Rodrigo gave him half a dose of the codeine pill the vet had supplied. That night the dog awakened every couple of hours, crying out. Rodrigo applied a warm towel to Blackie's belly, wrongly assuming that his trouble peeing was causing the discomfort. But that morning, Sami gave the dog a spoonful of olive oil and, eventually, the dog had a bowel movement and stopping crying. Sometimes, while the dog lay on the grass, it seemed to Rodrigo that Blackie was staring at some spot in the distance, seeing something or someone that only he, a dog, could see.

Once more, while Sami rested on the bed in the back of the van, Rodrigo spent most of the night on a wool blanket next to Blackie, getting up several times to tend to his dog. Neither he nor the dog got much sleep that night.

Chapter 18

In the early morning they arrived at the Atlantic coast and the large fishing-based city of Vigo which lay on a fjord-like bay, the Ria de Vigo. Rodrigo found parking near a dock and walked onto a wharf, past crates of barnacles, clams and oysters. He was passing a trawler off-loading its catch of sardines when he caught sight of his friend from school-days and waved at a short, dark-haired, clean-shaven young man wearing a brown turtleneck and a navy blue watch cap.

The fisherman came running, surprisingly fast in spite of his yellow oilskin lowers and rubber boots. When he was close, he stopped and unfastened the suspenders, pulled off his boots and stepped out of the waterproofs.

"Eh, Rodrigo. Good to see you."

"Toni!" he said, as they clasped hands in greeting. "Sorry to interrupt your work, but this is very, very important."

"Business?"

"It's getting more personal," he said, and explained the situation with his dog.

A look of concern crossed Toni's face. "I know how you feel. My dog died three months ago. I haven't gotten over it yet." He took a pair of ankle-high hiking boots from a canvas bag that was hooked on a nail set in the wharf's wooden railing and pulled them on. "So, what can I do for you?"

Rodrigo told his friend about Jorge Blanco's debt. "I'm running out of time on this, Toni. I gotta get Blackie back home."

Toni nodded. "I didn't see the guy, but someone on the crew pointed him toward that large vessel docked at the next pier, suggesting he might gain passage on it. It sails for North American waters at dawn tomorrow."

"Where did Blanco go?"

"After he left the ocean-going trawler, he was seen driving north. He'd mentioned visiting the place of pilgrimage, maybe to pass the time."

"Then that's where I'm headed."

"Wait up," Toni said. "My boat's scheduled for maintenance today. Let me clear it with the captain and I'll go with you. We'll grab this troublemaker."

The air washed onshore in a steady, cold wind. Gulls screeched overhead, looking to nab a free meal off the pier. The sound of waves crashing onto the rocky coastline was joined by the slap of water against the hulls of boats in the harbor.

Then there were the voices of fishermen hollering out in *gallego*, the language of Galicia, as their catch was hoisted over the side of trawlers. Billowy white clouds drifted in, promising rain soon and Rodrigo opened his mouth and tasted the salty air, ordinarily a treat for him. Unfortunately the small pleasures of life were becoming lost under a curtain of worry.

At the van, he introduced his friend. "Sami, this is Toni Pedrosa, the best deep sea fisherman of Seville."

"Probably the only one." Toni laughed. "We went to school together. He protected me from the bullies."

"Don't believe this guy. He boxed lightweight, never lost a match."

"How did you end up here?" she asked.

"Made the pilgrimage one year, married a local girl whose father owns a boat. So here I stayed." Toni's gray eyes twinkled.

"He knows the area and can help us find Blanco. Next stop, Santiago de Compostela."

Chapter 19

The toll road allowed for a fast pace to one of the Christian faith's greatest destinations for pilgrims. About an hour north of the fishing capital of the country, Santiago de Compostela had, long ago, become world-famous as the burial site of the bones of St. James, one of the three leading Apostles of Christ.

The other two in Christ's inner circle were St. John—his brother—and St. Peter, each of them a fisherman on the Sea of Galilee before Jesus of Nazareth called them to follow Him. The priceless relics were kept entombed in a crypt below the cathedral's main altar.

Since the Middle Ages, millions of pilgrims have made the journey to the Galician city. Many of them walked hundreds of miles from France, seeking spiritual renewal, an answer to prayer, to repay vows and promises, or for adventure. The numbers swelled with each passing year as the French route of pilgrimage became, for some, a fashionable trek to add to other globetrotting experiences.

In spite of the growth of "spiritual" tourism by non-believers, many pilgrims still made the trip for that oldest of reasons—a deep love of their Savior and Lord, and the chance to get close to the human remains of one of the "Sons of Thunder."

Rodrigo parked the van as close as possible to the Praza do Obradoiro, the main square onto which the cathedral faced. He placed the magnetic signs on the van again, not having used them since Valencia. Sami replaced the soiled pad under the dog with a dry one, and washed and dried his belly and hind legs of any blood or urine, while the men set off on foot into the vastness of the square.

He produced the photo of Jorge Blanco many times, showing it to street sweepers and other municipal workers, but not to policemen or tourists. No one recalled seeing the neatly-dressed professional man. Toni insisted that they enter the cathedral, though they skipped the tour group that had already started down the side aisle of the main sanctuary.

Toni gestured toward a white-haired priest arranging books near the high altar. "My wife's uncle. Let's talk to him."

When the priest saw Toni, a big smile broke over his rather severe-looking face and he came down the steps into the nave. "Toni, my son, what brings you here?"

"Father Juan, this is my best friend Rodrigo. He is searching for a man who is running from his responsibilities." Toni removed his watch cap, smoothed his hair and took the photo from Rodrigo's shirt pocket and held it out. "Have you seen him?"

The priest studied the picture. "He was here, not long ago. An educated man, by the way he spoke."

"What did he talk about, Father?"

"History, the crypt of St. James." The priest bowed his head in thought. "Oh, and he asked about Oviedo...the facecloth. He wanted to know if I thought it was genuine."

Toni glanced at Rodrigo. "Father, I have a special favor to ask."

"What is it, my son?"

"My friend's dog is dying. Would it be possible to bring the dog inside, near the bones of our blessed apostle? Perhaps a miracle of healing...?"

"Toni!" Rodrigo exclaimed.

The smile left the priest's face. "The Archbishop would disapprove. On the other hand, he is busy in Rome today." The smile returned. "Bring him to the Silversmith's Doorway. I will let you in."

Taking the wheel of the Mercedes van, Toni drove it by a roundabout route to the Praza das Praterias and parked by the stone fountain.

The fisherman went to the side door and knocked once and the priest opened the door. Rodrigo carried his ailing dog from the van into the cathedral. Cradling Blackie in his arms, he followed the priest. Toni and Sami walked quietly behind them. Flames flickered from a bank of votive candles, the high altar receiving the most light in the dimly-lit cathedral. The sense of worship and holiness was profound.

As in the Valencia church, the lingering scent of incense filled their nostrils. The tour group could be heard on the opposite end of the nave. Once again, Rodrigo felt humbled and out of his element. He felt the weight of his dog, now down to 55 pounds, but his arms and shoulders were not tired. Then they stood near the altar, under which the revered bones of the Apostle James rested.

The priest stepped back. "If anyone comes near, I will guide them away. Please, take your time."

Rodrigo knelt down, still holding his dog. While Toni stood near his relative, Sami moved up and placed a hand on Rodrigo's left shoulder, blocking the view of the dog from the people coming up the center aisle.

"Go ahead," she whispered, "say what's on your heart."

Rodrigo rolled his neck and stared at Blackie's head, which rested on his right forearm. "God, have mercy on my dog. You love him even more than I do. I don't expect he'll recover, not anymore. All I'm askin' is that he won't suffer. Take care of him, okay?"

He started to rise, struggled a bit, and then Sami and Toni each took an arm and lifted him and the dog up. Rodrigo bowed his head toward the altar and backed away. Fighting back tears, he told the priest, "Thanks, Father. I won't forget this."

The priest made the sign of the cross over Rodrigo and the dog. "In the name of the Father, and of the Son, and of the Holy Spirit. Go in peace, my son."

Outside, the glare of the sun had been replaced by a layer of dark clouds. The air smelled of rain coming in off the Atlantic, the first of autumn's many storms. They got into the van and, again, Toni drove until they had left the district of historic buildings. Sami sat up front beside Toni, looking back now and then at Rodrigo as he coaxed his dog to drink water.

Yesterday, Blackie had lifted his head at his master's approach. Now he just lay on his side, only the eyes moving. First thing each morning, Rodrigo took hope from the sight of the dog's chest and belly rising and falling. It meant that his dog was alive another day. But the respirations had slowed, the movement of his rib cage becoming less and less noticeable.

Toni borrowed Sami's cell phone and punched in a number. He spoke rapidly in the Galician language, listened for a minute and gave her back the phone. "Something's spooked your Senor Blanco," he told Rodrigo. "He called the trawler's captain and cancelled his booking, saying he'd catch a ferry instead of waiting."

"Santander. Sea-going ferry to Plymouth, England," Rodrigo guessed.

"He's got a few hours' head start. What's the plan?" Sami asked.

"We go after him. Keep it at 80 or 85 mph. We'll have to risk it." He ran his hand over the dog's right flank. "I don't care about a ticket, it's the time wasted by a traffic cop."

"We won't get pulled over," Toni promised.

Chapter 20

Before leaving Santiago de Compostela, Toni stopped at a small restaurant and returned to the van carrying a brown bag. He took out paper plates of grilled sardines and passed them out.

Sami and Rodrigo ate hungrily, savoring the locally-caught and perfectly-cooked fish, wiping up the remains with chunks of thick crusted bread dipped in olive oil.

Finished, Toni steered the Mercedes van onto the highway going northeast to meet the motorway along the coast, also known by pilgrims as the Northern Route in the many centuries before a modern superhighway was constructed.

Near the border with the province of Asturia, the road cut through a forested region where oak trees predominated, their green leaves changing to red and yellow as the month of September progressed. Sami noticed red squirrels scampering on the ground and up into the trees, collecting acorns.

The rocky hillsides of Galicia gave way to tree-covered rolling hills, although much of the land in this wet climate had been carved up into hay-growing pastures, as well as meadows for cattle grazing. Small farms bordered the highway, some of them extending very close to the wild surf that crashed onto rugged headlands off the Bay of Biscay, the heaving sea often in view to their left along the Costa Verde.

But the only sounds inside the van were that of the droning engine, tires slicing through water on the roadway, and the occasional splash from a passing vehicle. Toni kept the windshield wipers flicking back and forth.

Close to the town of Canero, Sami asked, "Any chance of passing through Oviedo?"

Toni shook his head. "We'd have to turn off onto a road to the southeast. This is the most direct route to Santander. What do you think, Rodrigo?"

"Why Oviedo?" Rodrigo asked Sami.

She held up her smartphone. "Picked up news of some kind of disturbance at the cathedral. It's the feast of San Mateo and the city is thronged with visitors. Let's just say I'm curious."

"You think Blanco is involved?"

"Not if he's as smart as you portrayed him—a university-educated professional. Then again, he's been on the run awhile, maybe stressed and tired and prone to making mistakes."

"Okay, Toni, make the turn southeast," Rodrigo said. "We'll check it out."

Toni swiveled his head, looked briefly at his friend and saw the fatigue eating at him. "Americans would call this a wild goose chase. We should press on to Santander or lose this guy to an international ferry."

"You're probably right," Rodrigo agreed. "It's just that Sami's been right a lot this week. Take the N634 for Oviedo."

Toni steered the van off the motorway onto the secondary road. "Attached to the cathedral is the Camara Santa, a private chapel that functions as a repository for priceless relics," he explained. "Some are so valuable, they are seldom put on display. The facecloth of Christ is kept there. It is often referred to as the Sudarium.

"According to some historical reports, the bloodstained cloth travelled from Jerusalem to North Africa, and entered Spain at Cartagena in the year 616. It was taken to Seville and, later, as the Moors advanced northward, brought to Asturias and hidden in a cave."

The rain stopped and he switched off the wipers. "This province resisted the Moors and, under its Visigothic king, Pelayo, defeated the Muslim army in 722 AD. Finally, a church was built to house the relic. It is recorded that in 1075, the Asturian king, his daughter and Rodrigo Diaz Vivar—also known as El Cid, the hero of the Reconquest—prayed and fasted before opening the Arca Santa, an oak chest which held the Sudarium, and viewed the sacred object. The king then ordered the chest encased in silver and kept in the Camara Santa, the Holy Chapel."

"I've heard of it," Sami said. "The church claims the cloth covered Jesus' face after the Crucifixion when He was laid out in the tomb, and that the Shroud of Turin was the cloth that covered His body. While both are objects of veneration, the Shroud receives more attention because of its size and the detailed image of a man captured in a negative photographic image. Although the authenticity of both is challenged, that isn't an obstacle for many believers."

She consulted her smartphone again and read from a digital version of the New Testament. "Joseph of Arimathea, a disciple of Jesus asked Pilate to let him take away the body from Golgotha, site of the Cross. When Pilate gave permission, Joseph and Nicodemus, two of Jesus' rare wealthy followers, came and took it. Nicodemus brought a mixture of one hundred pounds of myrrh and aloe, and they wrapped the dead body in cloths infused with the burial spices, following the custom of the Jews. There was a garden by the place of the Crucifixion, and in the garden was a tomb owned by Joseph. That is where they laid His body."

"No wonder many people travel to Oviedo," Toni said. "Otherwise it's just a medium-sized city with a university, museums, and Romanesque churches, not a place of spiritual pilgrimage—except for the three days a year when the facecloth is on public display."

Sami scrolled down on her phone and read, "Peter went straight into the tomb and saw the linen cloths on the ground, also the cloth that had covered his head—rolled up and set aside on its own. Then the other disciple went into the tomb and when he saw...he believed. Till then they had not understood the teaching of their Scriptures, that He must rise from the dead."

"The greatest moment in history," Toni said solemnly, and crossed himself.

Sami put down her phone. "The markings on the Shroud suggest that a body, at the atomic level, passed through the cloth, leaving an imprint. The marks—an image—left by blood on the facecloth are more indistinct."

"Still," Rodrigo noted, "you either choose to believe it is the real article or you don't. Most people on earth probably don't give it a thought. Others dismiss it as a religious superstition."

"People without imagination, people without a soul," Sami said. "They choose to believe there is no supernatural world and, for them, perhaps, they will get their wish."

"Then they are playing roulette with their lives, gambling there is nothing after death. If they are right, we are fools," Rodrigo said. "But what if they are wrong?"

"What I don't get," Toni mused, "is why Blanco would leave the motorway to Santander and drive toward a city that will be thronged with crowds for the fiesta."

"He's a man trained to evaluate numbers, a dispassionate occupation based on logic. Now he is into unfamiliar territory, physically and mentally, and he is giving way to panic," Rodrigo told his friend. "I've seen it happen before with amateurs. They leave with a plan, but when a complication arises they can't adapt and make the necessary adjustments."

"Wait a minute," Sami exclaimed. "Toni just told us that the Sudarium is available for viewing three days a year. Which days?"

"Good Friday," Toni said. "Then again on September 14, Feast of the Triumph of the Cross—"

"A week ago," she broke in. "What's the last day it is displayed each year?"

"September 21, the facecloth is brought out again."

"What's the date today?" Rodrigo asked.

Sami stared at her smartphone. "The 21st," she said softly. "That holy relic is being shown in the church right now."

Toni drove into the ancient Asturian city. Flashing blue lights filled the square in front of the Cathedral of the Holy Savior. Avoiding the crime or accident scene, he found a place to park in the vicinity of the Archeological Museum behind the cathedral. "Stay here while I ask around."

A few minutes later Toni was back, and climbed into the driver's seat. "National and local police are everywhere. There was an incident in the church. A man entered and demanded to touch the cloth, which is only about 33 inches by 21 inches. When a priest rejected the unusual request, the man threatened to set off a bomb.

"The police were called, and while the cathedral was evacuated the Sudarium was returned to its silver chest and taken back to the Camara Santa. In all the confusion, the intruder melted into the crowds."

"How'd you get all this info?" Sami asked.

Toni shrugged his shoulders. "My wife, Maria, comes from a large family. One of her cousins is with the Guardia Civil and a local cop knows him."

"Nothing like family connections."

"So what now?" Toni asked Rodrigo.

"Blanco's either gone crazy or he's pretty clever, creating a diversion. The latter seems out of character, but when a man is desperate enough..."

"On to Santander?"

"No. I don't think he'll try that now. He got off the motorway and headed south to this place. I've got a hunch he'll continue southward, try to throw us off."

"He knows he's being pursued?" Toni asked.

"He knows Don Miguel isn't going to let him escape easily. What would you do if you were on the run?"

Toni consulted the paper map. "Drive south through the mountains. From here, this guy can reach Castilla y Leon province, then make for Barcelona to the east or go south to Madrid. We'll take a motorway eastward and reconnect with the N634. Maybe another 25 miles to the national park. Keep in mind that, on mountain roads, he'll have an edge in his car if he's got any driving skill at all."

"Parque Nacional de los Picos de Europa," Sami said, looking over Toni's shoulder at the map. "For an accountant, he's taking some big risks."

"Maybe he was still in Santiago de Compostela when we arrived and saw us get down from the van," Toni suggested. "He knows he can outrun us when the road gets really twisty."

"Then he is more resourceful than I thought," Rodrigo admitted. "On the other hand, I doubt we've been recognized. He doesn't know me or my job in Don Miguel's organization. Look, I know we're not going to chase him down in an RV. I just want to stay close, because he *will* slip up."

Chapter 21

Rodrigo sat cross-legged on the floor of the van, the black lab's head resting on his lap. He'd just changed the absorbent pad. The dog was still losing blood while urinating and no longer lifted his head on his own. Rodrigo feared that life was slipping away from his beloved friend and there was nothing he could do about it.

Sami looked back and started to say something, then bit her lower lip. What could she say that would help? she wondered. But she had no answer to her unspoken question.

The sharp, jutting peaks of the Picos de Europa range loomed ahead and Toni skillfully took the Mercedes van onto a narrow winding road up into the mountains of the national park. Still well below the tree line, they passed stands of beech, birch and rowans, the leaves changing color, as in the lowlands. The park provided habitat for most of the country's remaining brown bears, as well as wolves—animals seldom seen near the roads, or even by hikers on backcountry trails.

The road curved sharply around limestone hills in a series of switchbacks leading up toward a pass through the highest peaks, many still capped with snow. Occasionally visible was the tallest mountain in Spain, at about 8000 feet. On the side of the road, rugged gorges plunged menacingly downward off of steep, jagged cliffs. Once they were into the higher elevations, low clouds descended and limited visibility for a while, until the heavy gray mist suddenly parted for a hundred yards or more and then, just as abruptly, closed in again. Coming out of a particularly nasty patch of wet fog, they found a relatively straight and clear stretch of blacktop, with a blind curve a quarter of a mile ahead.

Rodrigo said urgently, "Pull over, Toni. Find a place and pull over. Now!"

Toni eased off the accelerator and gradually braked to a stop, half on the road, half on green grass. The grass sloped down on their right for a few yards before dropping, precipitously, over a hundred feet to rocks below. "What is it, Rodrigo. What's wrong?"

"The dog," Sami said quietly. "It's his dog."

Tears streamed down Rodrigo's face. He didn't bother to wipe them away. He was kneeling by Blackie's head as the dog ground its teeth. Gently he pried open its mouth to push the tongue back inside, free of the canines and incisors. Then the dog's legs stiffened in a kind of spasm—first the hind legs, then the forelegs—before relaxing a bit.

Finally Blackie arched his neck and howled quietly, just once, and lowered his head. Rodrigo risked a glance at the dog's chest and flank and saw that the rise and fall of respiration had stopped. He put a hand in front of the lab's big and beautiful black nose but felt no air from the nostrils. Blackie was no longer breathing.

"He's gone," Rodrigo whispered.

"*Vaya con Dios*," Toni said, and bowed his head.

"I'm going to miss you, boy." Rodrigo watched the dog's brown eyes, now unmoving. Slowly he ran his hands over the dog's soft chest hair and caressed its head. "I can't believe you're really gone."

Chapter 22

Holding back tears, Sami opened the door and slid down from the passenger seat. She wanted to cry alone for her new friend's loss. Plus, she too had loved Blackie.

Knowing the dog for only a week, she'd come to cherish his company and had thrown herself into caring for him. Now he was dead. Her heart ached for Rodrigo. Aimlessly, she wandered off the grass and into the road in front of the RV.

It was the sound of tires screeching—losing traction on the damp road—that caught her ear. But when she looked around, there wasn't a vehicle in sight. She brushed away the tears from her cheeks and walked down the road, the fingertips of her left hand trailing along the side of the red van.

Then she heard the whine of an engine, drawing nearer, and she glanced back and saw a black car racing around the blind bend, accelerating hard.

For a moment she couldn't think straight and stood still, frozen with indecision. Suddenly a cold fear gripped her and she turned away from the speeding car and moved toward the back of the van.

She almost made it when the car's left front fender clipped her right leg and sent her bouncing off the Mercedes' sheet metal, spinning her around and onto the unyielding road surface. That's when the car's driver lost control and the vehicle skidded onto the grass, tearing ruts into the soft dirt before it spun around and went backwards down the slope and flipped over.

Not far away, Sami lay facedown and absolutely motionless.

Toni was first out of the van. "I know it's a bad time for you," he told his grieving friend, "but Sami's hurt."

Rodrigo left his dog, opened the sliding door and ran to the back on the passenger side. "Check the car and driver," he said to Toni, and dropped to his knees beside Sami. He started to raise her head off the wet grass and felt a flat rock underneath. Knocked out cold, he realized, and taking extra care, turned her onto her back and checked her breathing. "Nothing," he muttered to himself. Pressing two fingers to her neck, he felt for a pulse. "No pulse, either. Come on, Sami, I can't lose you, too!"

Carefully, he pulled her bulky sweater up to her neck and began CPR. "Two breaths and fifteen chest compressions," he said aloud.

Toni stood close by, watching the road for traffic. "I'll try to call for an ambulance, okay?"

"Can you get a signal up here?" Rodrigo pressed both hands down on Sami's chest near her breastbone.

"What about the driver of the car?"

"If she doesn't make it, he'll wish he'd died in the crash," Rodrigo pronounced grimly. "Yeah, try and make the call."

"Let me know if you want to switch places." Toni ran to grab the phone and punched in 091 for the *Policia Nacional* to request a *Cruz Roja* ambulance. After a few seconds, he said, "We're out of mobile range, probably blocked by the mountains."

Tilting her chin up, Rodrigo blew two breaths, checked for a pulse again and went back to performing chest compressions.

Toni glanced anxiously up and down the road. "The cops are never around when you need them. How's she doing?"

"Come on, Sami, help me out here!" he pleaded, and looked up. "Four minutes, tops. Otherwise it's not good at all, even if we bring her back. Brain damage, like a stroke or dementia."

Suddenly Sami's hands jerked and her eyes opened halfway.

"Oh, God," Rodrigo cupped the back of her head with his right hand, "you're alive."

She gulped deep breaths of the cold air. "I was there," she gasped.

"Yes," he said, "you're here with us. Spain...the mountains."

"You don't understand. I saw him." She closed her eyes for a few seconds, as if trying to recapture an image from a dream. When she re-opened her blue and brown eyes, she said softly, "I saw your dog. I saw Blackie in Heaven."

"She's hallucinating," Toni said. "We've got to get her into the van, out of the cold."

"I saw him, Rodrigo," she insisted. "It's not my imagination. You've got to believe me."

"I believe you, sweetheart. But first, show me you can move your legs."

She turned her feet from side to side, then bent her legs at the knees.

"Good. Now your arms."

Sami flexed her arms and then, as she tried to lift her head, winced.

"Sorry, I had to make sure your spine wasn't injured." Gently, he lift-ed her off the road and carried her past the dog's body, and laid her on the bed in back of the van.

"You've suffered a concussion, a bad one," he said, and covered her with a wool blanket. He didn't tell her that she had been clinically dead for a couple of minutes.

"I'm gonna turn your head to the left to check where it hit, Sami. I know it feels sore, but I gotta see for myself."

"I went through a dark tunnel," she said hoarsely, "and there was this unbelievably bright light at the end of it."

He took the first aid kit, opened an antiseptic packet and, after cleaning the wound caused by the impact with the rock, wiped her face with a warm, damp towel that Toni had heated in the microwave. "You need to rest. For pain we'll go with aspirin."

Toni cautioned, "If there's a head injury, better skip the aspirin. It thins the blood, may increase internal bleeding. What else you got?"

"The vet prescribed Tylenol 4 for Blackie."

"That'll work for now, until we get her to the closest hospital's casualty department." Toni went to the front of the van. "I'm going down the slope, check on the driver. I mean, it could've been an accident."

Chapter 23

"Skip the pills," Sami told Rodrigo. "My neck and head are sore, but I'll live."

"No kidding? Welcome back to the land of the living."

"Don't you dare try to humor me."

He decided to spell it out. "We lost you for a while, know what I mean?"

"I know that, Rodrigo. It was like I was floating above the van, watching my own body as it lay on the road while that car flew over the edge. Then I was pulled through the tunnel." She blinked her eyes. "I'm not making this up."

Rodrigo nodded, looked over his shoulder at Blackie. "I've read about such things. Near death experiences—NDE's they're called."

"My whole life flashed before my eyes, like in a movie. Everything I'd said and done passed before me."

He patted her brow with the cloth. "So you don't want a pill for the pain? Fine, we'll see what a doctor thinks."

"You're not listening to me! I'm telling you that I saw Blackie. He looked different...and yet the same. It's hard to explain." She tried to sit up, groaned and lay back down. "His head didn't have those ridges on top. It was broad and flat. His back and hips were full, no longer shrunken. He was running and jumping, his tongue hanging out, as if to say, 'See, I'm all right now.'"

Rodrigo tried to smile. "It's okay, you're tired."

"There were others there to meet me. People I've never seen before."

"Sure, kiddo. Can you describe them?"

"You still don't get it? Okay, there was a man who resembled you, only he looked about ten years older. I could see that from his eyes. But his face was without wrinkles, a good, strong face. He wore one of those flat-topped, broad-brimmed hats men wear in Andalusia, and he was dressed in a black suit and a white shirt, but not for church-going or a funeral. It had the feel of a festival, like a feast day."

She paused while he put down the towel. "Nearby stood a lady in a white and red dress, the kind flamenco dancers wear, all fluffy and frilly with extra cloth at the shoulders. She looked like an Andalusian woman at a fiesta."

Rodrigo studied her intently. "She wore a black *mantilla*?"

"Now you are testing me," Sami said sharply. "No, no *mantilla*. She held a black wooden fan. It looked hand-carved and was decorated with many dark pink violets."

Rodrigo sat up straight. "Did you see her face?"

"Mostly the right side. The fan hid the rest...except, she lowered the fan briefly, as if she wanted me to see something."

"And what did you see?"

"A birthmark, extending from her left cheekbone into her eye. Rodrigo, she was the most beautiful woman I have ever seen."

He got up, shook his head a few times, and sat down again. "It can't be," he said quietly, "it simply cannot be."

"What's wrong?"

"My mother...you saw my mother. But, how could you know?"

"Know what?"

"I have only one photograph of my parents and they are dressed as you have described. I keep it locked in a trunk in my bedroom. As for the fan—the flowers painted on it grow only in the Sierra de Cazorla mountains in eastern Andalusia where she was born. The fan is in the trunk, too."

"I'd like to see the fan. And the picture."

"You don't understand," he said, and cleared his throat. "The photo shows her in profile, right side only. Although I was young when they died, I remember everything about her. She used to sing me to sleep. I would look into her eyes while she sang. She had that reddish birthmark, just as you saw."

Sami began to sob. "Now do you believe what I have told you?"

"Forgive me for doubting."

"Your dog is in Heaven, Rodrigo. And there were other animals—cats, goats, horses, even wild creatures and birds. It is the loveliest place, more beautiful than you can imagine."

"Did you touch him?"

"No. But he looked at me and it's like I could read his mind. He was telling me that you should not worry. He will see you again."

At that, Rodrigo covered his face with his hands and wept.

Just then, Toni stuck his head through the sliding doorway. "You won't believe this. The driver is that Blanco guy we were after. I checked his wallet and it's him. He's trapped in the car, hanging upside down from his seatbelt. He swears he wasn't trying to hit the girl—claims he tried to brake and skidded out of control. He thought he'd gotten away from us, but the fog closed in ahead and he couldn't see where he was going, so he turned back." Toni pointed toward the wrecked car. "He's not going anywhere until the police or fire brigade pry him out. I'll try the mobile again."

Chapter 24

In silence, Toni drove the van back to Vigo.

Rodrigo sat on the floor next to his dog. He had covered Blackie with a wool blanket, determined to be respectful of the animal's body, though he badly wanted to see his companion again. A couple of times they stopped to break the journey and he lifted up the blanket and gazed at his friend, who looked peaceful in death, almost like he was just taking a nap. Even though Rodrigo knew his dog wouldn't wake up, not in this world, he felt an assurance—the promise that they would be reunited someday.

After heartfelt goodbyes, Toni offered a piece of advice. "Another one of my wife's cousins," he said, grinning, "is a monk at the Monasterio de Oseira, here in Galicia, not fifteen miles off your route. In addition to prayer and his other duties as a Trappist monk, he provides a shelter for abused animals. Stop by and talk with him."

"Perhaps another time. I want to get back home and, you know..."

"I'll call ahead and warn him you're coming."

From her bed in back, Sami asked, "Aren't members of that order forbidden to speak? Don't they take a vow of silence or something?"

"He'll get special permission. Just ask for Brother Sebastian."

"All right, we'll stop by the monastery for a few minutes." Rodrigo switched over to the driver's seat. "Thanks for all your help, Toni."

"Your Jorge Blanco will be a long time in the hospital at Oviedo under police guard, recovering from broken bones and internal bleeding. He'll be charged with dangerous driving and will probably do jail time for it." The fisherman pulled his watch cap on. "Looks like Don Miguel will have to wait his turn for this guy."

Rodrigo waved and drove away from the wharves of Vigo. The drive was uneventful on the A52 east. He easily found the turning north onto another motorway and then left the highway several miles later for a secondary road that led into the forested hills around the Valle de Arenteiro.

The grey stone walls of the monastery dated to 1137 AD, the orange tile roof of more recent vintage. It was a large compound with a two-towered church, cloisters and a columned courtyard. Additionally, there was an extensive library, as well as a lapidarium containing stones and material from the monastery's earliest years.

Before the main building, the road veered left to some smaller outbuildings, including one where bandaged goats and horses grazed on grass in front of an old stone house. After parking the van on a dirt driveway, Rodrigo went back to Sami.

"The doc in Oviedo wants you to rest, so stay here."

She started to pull off the blanket. "Other than an aching neck and bad headache, I'm doing great."

"Oh? What about those bruises on your hip and leg?"

"Nothing broken."

"I seem to remember the doc had x-rays taken. He said you sustained severe contusions to your thigh and hip, black and blue that'll turn yellow—"

"Okay, okay," she tried to get up and grimaced, "it feels excruciatingly sore. Satisfied now?"

"You almost died, Sami Zafzaf. In fact, clinically, you *were* dead."

She stared at the ceiling, lost in thought for a moment. "It wasn't scary like I thought it'd be. I'm not afraid of dying anymore, now that I know there's a better place waiting for us."

He looked down the aisle at the blanket covering Blackie. "Toni really wants me to meet this Brother Sebastian, so that's what I'm going to do. I won't be long."

"I heard him tell Sebastian's story. This monk actually killed a guy?"

"He was with the Guardia Civil in Cantabria Province. There was a border incident with Basque separatists and Sebastian shot one. The man died on the way to the hospital. Sebastian was badly wounded in the shootout and, after recovering, left the police force and joined the Trappist Order."

"A life of action exchanged for a life of prayer."

"That's what Toni asked his relative. Sebastian replied that, contrary to most people's perception, much of his police work was surveillance—watching and waiting. In some ways, a life of prayer isn't really so different. And then there is his active work, rescuing animals."

"He sounds like a good man," she said. "I'd like to meet him."

"Maybe you will. But for now, stay put and rest."

Leaving the van, he heard dogs barking inside the house and, without knocking, opened the front door and stepped inside.

Chapter 25

Wearing a white wool habit—with a long black cloth draped around his shoulders and a large silver cross hanging from a chain onto his chest—the monk turned to inspect his visitor, then continued clipping the nails of a small, scraggly dog, its fur matted, chunks of hair missing.

The house was actually one large room; in effect, a kennel. Cats and dogs lay in hand-built wooden and wire enclosures of varying sizes, grooming themselves or resting. Some of the dogs barked, but not constantly. None of the animals whined. There were also rabbits and, in one cage, what looked like a weasel.

Some animals wore white bandages on their limbs, like those outside. Rodrigo felt he had entered a clinic on Noah's Ark. The smell was tolerable, not at all offensive, and the floor was clean. Each animal had a water bowl.

"Brother Sebastian? I am Rodrigo de Lorca, Toni's friend."

"Welcome to my shelter," the monk replied. His head was not shaved in the tonsorial cut seen on many monks; rather, he had a full head of longish dark hair. Physically, he was of above average height with a solid physique. "Toni alerted me about your situation. I am sorry to hear that your dog has passed on."

"Thank you," Rodrigo said, and coughed. "I'm not exactly sure what I'm doing here."

"Please, sit down." The monk indicated a tall wooden stool and lifted the little dog, rubbed his fur and put him into one of the hand-built crates. "These creatures," he waved an arm around the room, "are my family and my congregation. I serve them and, in return, they teach me about life and God's love."

Rodrigo said nothing. If he hadn't known of Sebastian's prior life, the monk's introduction might've seemed a little silly. But here was a man who had risked everything in service to his country. It was obvious that the man had a reservoir of wisdom worth listening to.

"We are all at a different stage in our spiritual journeys," Brother Sebastian continued. "You have suffered a great loss and your heart is sad and you are wondering if you will ever see your dog again. Am I correct in assuming this?"

"I miss him very much," Rodrigo said.

"Do you believe in God?"

"I was baptized into the Roman Catholic church."

The monk picked up a bowl of dry cat food and went from cage to cage, distributing it to the waiting felines. "What I am asking is, do you believe in Jesus Christ our Lord and Savior, in the forgiveness of sins and in the life everlasting? In other words, can you accept the words of Holy Scripture as true and meant to inform us in our belief and conduct?"

Rodrigo thought for a minute. "I want to believe. But sometimes it is difficult to see God at work in my life. The truth is, I am not a good example of a Christian."

"Listen to His words from the Book of Job. 'If you wish to learn, ask the cattle and gather knowledge from the birds. Those that crawl will teach you lessons, the creatures of the ocean will explain everything. All creatures know this world is of God, that He sustains the soul of everything that lives, and gives us the breath of life.' Now, I am paraphrasing, not quoting exactly, but the meaning is clear to those willing to learn."

"Please, go on."

"Psalm 50 tells us that 'every animal in the forest, all the birds flying through the air, everything moving in the fields belongs to the Lord.'

And from the Book of Revelation, 'All creatures in the air, above the ground and under the ground and in the oceans cried out in praise to the One sitting on the throne and to the Lamb of God.' You see, Rodrigo, Almighty God created the animals and they live because of Him, just as you and I do."

Brother Sebastian set down the bowl, unlatched an enclosure and took out a white and brown cat. "When God was so disappointed at the depravity of the human race in the days of Noah, He planned to destroy the Earth and all that was in it. When He spared us through Noah, He also made sure that animals would survive. They were brought, two by two, into the ark to repopulate the planet after the flood. In the world to come, animals will have their place, too."

"The lion shall lie down with the lamb," Rodrigo said.

The monk smiled. "Close enough. The verse from the Book of Isaiah actually says, 'The wolf shall dwell with the lamb.'" Putting the injured cat back in its crate, he nodded toward the other animals. "It is a glorious picture of God's plan for us and for them."

The sounds of an organ, skillfully played, entered the room and Rodrigo asked, "I am keeping you from worship?"

"Brother Joaquin is practicing. Before joining the order, he was principal organist at Madrid's Cathedral de la Almudena."

"You have tried to reassure me and I am grateful."

"If the hope of seeing our animal friends in the next life is false, then the words of Scripture are lies and our Holy Savior was either a liar or a lunatic...or both. But our faith and the Scriptures—in effect, a history book filled with eyewitness accounts—tells us that cannot possibly be so. Personally, I think it is usually a man or woman trying to hide or deny sin who challenges the truth of our faith. It isn't so much intellectual objections as it is moral ones."

"I hadn't thought of that."

Warming to the subject, the monk declared, "Much of modern language is used for deceitful purposes, the worst of which is self-deception. Nowadays, when people do something wrong, they don't repent. Instead, they proclaim 'I can't talk about it, I'm moving on,' while stylish people explain that they are 'going forward,' as if this is the most modern of virtues." Brother Sebastian sighed. "People make mistakes. God forgives. There is hope for all."

"I want to go back, back to the days when Blackie and I took long walks together."

"Then you are a man of character. Our memories are part of who we are." The monk walked along a row of enclosures, pouring clean water into small ceramic bowls. "When something tragic occurs, say the death of a child, the parents are encouraged to seek closure.

"But for such a loss, there can be no complete end to the pain in their heart, not in this world. How can it be otherwise? For with great love comes great joy and, unfortunately, the risk of great sorrow. It is part of life in this suffering world."

"You speak wisely, Brother Sebastian," Rodrigo said, and got off the stool. "Do you accept donations for this work?"

"Only through my order." The monk went to the door. "May I see your dog?"

Rodrigo led the way, opened the sliding door and pointed to the form under the blanket.

Brother Sebastian climbed in, knelt beside the dog and pulled back the blanket. He laid hands on Blackie's head and prayed silently. Then he drew out a glass vial from a hidden pocket and sprinkled drops onto the dog. Again he prayed and, after covering Blackie with the blanket, climbed down from the van. "He was your faithful friend and companion. Now he waits for you."

"Rodrigo clasped the brother's arm and squeezed it. "Gracias. I am very grateful for your time and prayers."

Chapter 26

On the following day, under a warm afternoon sun, Rodrigo dug a grave under the gnarled branches of the old olive tree where Blackie had often lain down in the shade. Then, from the cottage, he carried the body of his dog in his arms to a spot of grass nearby.

The rigor mortis had subsided and the dog, while not as supple as when he still breathed, looked like he was sleeping. As Sami watched from a reclining wicker chair that he had set down for her near the tree, he wrapped Blackie in a white sheet, taking extra care to cover his eyes, ears and nose from the dirt, and placed him in the grave.

Leaning on the shovel, he said, "Lord, thanks for this dog's life, his loyal friendship. I'll miss him. Goodbye for now, my friend."

Finally, without speaking, he shovelled dirt over the sheet until the hole was filled in and set a rough wooden cross at the head of the soft mound.

"Blackie," Sami said, reading the word he'd painted on the cross. She wiped away a tear. "At the monastery I fell asleep. Why didn't you wake me?"

"You slept because you were tired."

"I wanted to meet Brother Sebastian."

"We'll go back there." He looked steadily into her blue and brown eyes. "That is, unless you're returning to Morocco."

From the far side of the olive grove came a bark, a single deep bark that carried on the wind, lodged in their ears and drifted away.

She asked, "Are you going to be okay?"

"I prayed for a miracle."

"The Holy Grail, the remains of St. James...we tried our best."

He rested the shovel against the tree trunk. "I found out that God answered my prayer, just not the way I wanted."

"What do you mean?"

"I was scared of losing my dog and hoped God would heal him. But Blackie was already very ill and God took him home. You said that you saw him there, in that better place."

"Your dog is playing in the fields of the Lord."

A slight smile broke across Rodrigo's face. "What happened at Valencia and Santiago de Compostela were miracles. I believe that God is healing my heart. That is the answer to my prayers." He sat on the ground beside her. "I'm not alone now, am I?"

"No, not alone." She put a hand on his shoulder. "I am here as long as you like."

"Someday there'll be another dog running between the trees, barking and chasing wild rabbits. I think Blackie will like that."

The End of this story.
And, for Blackie, a new beginning.
In memory of a black Lab named Scooby.